Pat Hobby and Orson Welles
and Other Short Stories

Dans la même collection

Lire en anglais

Thirteen Modern English and American Short Stories

Roald Dahl : Someone Like You and Other Short Stories

Somerset Maugham : The Escape and Other Short Stories

F. Scott Fitzgerald : Pat Hobby and Orson Welles and Other Short Stories

Lire en allemand

Moderne Erzählungen

Deutsche Kurtzgeschichten

Lire en espagnol

Cuentos selectos

Cuentos del mundo hispánico

LIRE EN ANGLAIS
Collection dirigée par Henri Yvinec

F. Scott Fitzgerald

Pat Hobby and Orson Welles and Other Short Stories

Choix et annotations par Martine Skopan
Agrégée de l'Université

Le Livre de Poche

Sommaire

Tout naturellement, après quelques années d'étude d'une langue étrangère, naît l'envie de découvrir sa littérature. Mais, par ailleurs, le vocabulaire dont on dispose est souvent insuffisant. La perspective de recherches lexicales multipliées chez le lecteur isolé, la présentation fastidieuse du vocabulaire, pour le professeur, sont autant d'obstacles redoutables. C'est pour tenter de les aplanir que nous proposons cette nouvelle collection.

Celle-ci constitue une étape vers la lecture autonome, sans dictionnaire ni traduction, grâce à des notes facilement repérables. S'agissant des élèves de lycée, les ouvrages de cette collection seront un précieux instrument pédagogique pour les enseignants en langues étrangères puisque les recommandations pédagogiques officielles (Bulletin officiel de l'Éducation nationale du 9 juillet 1987) les invitent à "faire de l'entraînement à la lecture individuelle une activité régulière" qui pourra aller jusqu'à une heure hebdomadaire. Ces recueils de textes devraient ainsi servir de complément à l'étude de la civilisation.

Le lecteur trouvera donc :

En page de gauche

Des textes contemporains choisis pour leur intérêt littéraire et la qualité de leur langue.

En page de droite

Des notes juxtalinéaires rédigées dans la langue du texte, qui aident le lecteur à

Comprendre

Tous les mots et expressions difficiles contenus dans la ligne de gauche sont reproduits en caractères gras et expliqués dans le contexte.

Observer
Des notes d'observation de la langue soulignent le caractère idiomatique de certaines tournures ou constructions.

Apprendre
Dans un but d'enrichissement lexical, certaines notes proposent enfin des synonymes, des antonymes, des expressions faisant appel aux mots qui figurent dans le texte.

Grammaire au fil des nouvelles

Chaque nouvelle est suivie de phrases de thème inspirées du texte avec références à celui-ci pour le corrigé. En les traduisant le lecteur, mis sur la voie par des italiques et/ou des amorces d'explication, révise les structures rebelles les plus courantes ; cette petite "grammaire en contexte" est fondée sur la fréquence des erreurs.

Vocabulaire en contexte

En fin de volume une liste d'un millier de mots contenus dans les nouvelles, suivis de leur traduction, comporte, entre autres, les verbes irréguliers et les mots qui n'ont pas été annotés faute de place ou parce que leur sens était évident dans le contexte. Grâce à ce lexique on pourra, en dernier recours, procéder à quelques vérifications ou faire un bilan des mots retenus au cours des lectures.

The eight stories of this book belong to the Pat Hobby sequence, which comprises seventeen. Those were first published as a complete collection in 1962 by Scribner's. They had all originally appeared in the American magazine *Esquire* between 1939 and 1941. When Francis Scott Fitzgerald died in December 1940, two-thirds had been published. The last stories were thus published after his death.

The first he had sent for publication was *A Man in the Way*. It was about Pat Hobby, the 'scenario hack' as he called him. Then came a second *Boil Some Water, Lots of it*. The first five stories were written in under one month. There were also many revised versions. To the day he died, he kept shuffling the order of appearance of the stories. His final choice has been followed in this edition.

F. S. Fitzgerald was then working as a writer at Universal Studios in Hollywood. He wrote screenplays (in collaboration), among which *Three Comrades*, produced by Joseph Mankiewicz. The reason he had come to Hollywood in the first place was that he had to pay his debts (particularly to his literary agent Harold Ober). He was so short of money still that he needed the extra cash he could get from the Pat Hobby stories. He would write a first version of the story, send it to Arnold Gingrich of *Esquire* for approval, ask for the money to be wired to him in California in advance of publication, then write a revised version. It must be noted that at the same time he was working on his last novel, *The Last Tycoon* (published posthumously in 1941), which would dwell on many of the same themes.

How far is Pat Hobby a portrait of Fitzgerald himself? Though he would refer to himself as a hack writer, he was never in such disastrous circumstances as his hero was. On one occasion, he was even hired to adapt one of his own stories *Babylon Revisited*. But he was so dependent on the money to support his mentally sick wife and to send his daughter to college that being out of work even a short period made him anxious.

Besides, he was in poor health while writing the stories (bouts of fever and two heart attacks) and the descriptions of Pat's rheumy joints are certainly genuine.

But the main likeness between the two is alcoholism. Though Fitzgerald was at that time on the wagon, he had in the past shared Pat's craving for whisky when things got too difficult for him to handle. Passing allusions to Pat's little pocket flask arouse the readers' sympathy and pity more than their disgust.

All in all then the stories are not an accurate account of

F.S. Fitzgerald in Hollywood. It is a tongue-in-cheek description of the world of Hollywood in its heyday, at times cynical, always funny, its cruelty tempered with mercy for poor Pat. F. S. Fitzgerald had initially written the Pat Hobby stories to keep the wolf from the door, but he got so interested in his unlikely hero that he succeeded in creating an enduring type. His talent features a wonderful ear for dialogue, a sharp eye for a scene and a limpid and beautiful prose style. It is also the story of an industry, the motion-picture business, that he would observe at close range in *The Last Tycoon*.

F. S. FITZGERALD : A CHRONOLOGY

1896: born in Saint-Paul, Minnesota
1913: enters Princeton
1915: drops out of Princeton in December
1917: joins the Army as Second Lieutenant
1918: meets Zelda Sayre, his future wife
1919: takes job with advertising agency
sells short story to *Saturday Evening Post*
1920: Scribner's publishes *This Side of Paradise*
marriage to Zelda
1921: first trip to Europe
birth of his only daughter Scottie
1922: *The Beautiful and Damned* published
1924: second trip abroad
1925: *The Great Gatsby* published
meets Ernest Hemingway
1930: Zelda Fitzgerald breaks down
1932: Zelda Fitzgerald's second breakdown
1934: her third breakdown
Tender is the Night published
1937: working in Hollywood for M.G.M.
1939: first hapter of *The Last Tycoon*
1940: dies December

F. S. Fitzgerald as a short story writer:
There have been various collections of short stories. Some of the most famous of his short stories are: *May Day* (1920), *Bernice Bobs her Hair* (1920), *The Diamond as Big as the Ritz* (1922), *Babylon Revisited* (1931), *The Lost Decade* (1939). Autobiographical pieces include *The Crack-Up* (1936).

A MAN IN THE WAY

Pat Hobby could always get on the lot. He had worked there fifteen years on and off — chiefly off during the past five — and most of the studio police knew him. If tough customers on watch asked to see his studio card he could get in by phoning Lou, the bookie. For Lou also, the studio had been home for many years.

Pat was forty-nine. He was a writer but he had never written much, nor even read all the 'originals' he worked from, because it made his head bang to read much. But the good old silent days you got somebody's plot and a smart secretary and gulped benzedrine 'structure' at her six or eight hours every week. The director took care of the gags. After talkies came he always teamed up with some man who wrote dialogue. Some young man who liked to work.

'I've got a list of credits second to none,' he told Jack Berners. 'All I need is an idea and to work with somebody who isn't all wet.'

He had buttonholed Jack outside the production office as Jack was going to lunch and they walked together in the direction of the commissary.

'You bring *me* an idea,' said Jack Berners. 'Things are tight. We can't put a man on salary unless he's got an idea.'

'How can you get ideas off salary?' Pat demanded — then he added hastily: 'Anyhow I got the germ of an idea that I could be telling you all about at lunch.'

Something might come to him at lunch. There was Baer's notion about the boy scout. But Jack said cheerfully:

'I've got a date for lunch, Pat. Write it out and send it around, eh?'

get: come into ☐ **lot:** studio
on and off: irregularly ☐ **chiefly off:** most often not working
five: five years ☐ **tough customers on watch:** entrance guards who were more strict ☐ **card:** permit
get in: get into the studio ☐ **bookie:** man who takes people's money to bet on horses ☐ **home:** like his home
writer: script writer
nor even: *ni même* ☐ **original:** first version of scenario
made his head bang: gave him a headache
silent days: the days of silent movies ☐ **plot:** story
smart: clever ☐ **gulped benzedrine structure:** dictated with effort a scenario created with help of stimulant ☐ **director:** who directed the film ☐ **talkies:** talking films ☐ **teamed up:** collaborated

credits: *génériques* ☐ **second to none:** surpassed by no other
all: the only thing
who isn't all wet: who knows the job
he had buttonholed Jack: he had stopped Jack to speak to him
as: when ☐ **going to lunch:** going to have lunch
commissary: cafeteria
bring: to bring, brought, brought
tight: difficult ☐ **put... on salary:** employ ☐ **unless:** except if

off salary: if you are not employed (and paid)
hastily: quickly ☐ **anyhow:** in any case ☐ **got:** have got

something might come to him: he might have an idea
notion: idea
cheerfully: happily, good-humouredly
I've got a date: I'm meeting someone ☐ **write it out:** put it on paper
send... around: send it to my office

He felt cruel because he knew Pat couldn't write anything out but he was having story trouble himself. The war had just broken out and every producer on the lot wanted to end their current stories with the hero going to war. And Jack Berners felt he had thought of that first for his production.

'So write it out, eh?'

When Pat didn't answer Jack looked at him — he saw a sort of whipped misery in Pat's eye that reminded him of his own father. Pat had been in the money before Jack was out of college — with three cars and a chicken over every garage. Now his clothes looked as if he'd been standing at Hollywood and Vine for three years.

'Scout around and talk to some of the writers on the lot,' he said. 'If you can get one of them interested in your idea, bring him up to see me.'

'I hate to give an idea without money on the line,' Pat brooded pessimistically. 'These young squirts'll lift the shirt off your back.'

They had reached the commissary door.

'Good luck, Pat. Anyhow we're not in Poland.'

— Good *you're* not, said Pat under his breath. They'd slit your gizzard.

Now what to do? He went up and wandered along the cell block of writers. Almost everyone had gone to lunch and those who were in he didn't know. Always there were more and more unfamiliar faces. And he had thirty credits; he had been in the business, publicity and script-writing, for twenty years.

The last door in the line belonged to a man he didn't like. But he wanted a place to sit a minute so with a knock

story trouble: problems with a scenario ☐ **war:** *guerre*
broken out: to break, broke, broken ☐ **producer:** who plans and finances films ☐ **current stories:** the films they were working on then ☐ **thought of that first:** been the first to have the idea
production: film

when: as ☐ **saw:** to see, saw, seen
whipped: hurt, persecuted ☐ **misery:** unhappiness ☐ **reminded:** made him think ☐ **in the money:** rich, successful
college: university ☐ **chicken:** girl (American slang)

standing: staying ☐ **Hollywood and Vine:** the corner of Hollywood Boulevard and Vine Boulevard
scout around: try and get information
interested: interested in
bring him up: take him to my office
hate: dislike ☐ **money on the line:** being paid without delay
brooded: with a depressed look ☐ **squirts:** *blancs-becs*
lift the shirt off your back: steal your ideas and pretend they are their ideas ☐ **reached:** arrived at, come to
anyhow: at least
under his breath: without being heard
slit your gizzard: cut your throat, kill you
what to do: what could he do ☐ **wandered:** walked slowly
cell block: writers' offices which looked like prison cells
who were in: who were working in their offices
thirty credits: his name had appeared thirty times in the credits
in the business: working in films

belonged to: was that of
with a knock: knocking on the door

he pushed it open. The man wasn't there — only a very pretty, frail-looking girl sat reading a book.

'I think he's left Hollywood,' she said in answer to his question. 'They gave me his office but they forgot to put up my name.'

'You a writer?' Pat asked in surprise.

'I work at it.'

'You ought to get 'em to give you a test.'

'No — I like writing.'

'What's that you're reading.'

She showed him.

'Let me give you a tip,' he said. 'That's not the way to get the guts out of a book.'

'Oh.'

'I've been here for years — I'm Pat Hobby — and I *know*. Give the book to four of your friends to read it. Get them to tell you what stuck in their minds. Write it down and you've got a picture — see?'

The girl smiled.

'Well, that's very — very original advice, Mr. Hobby.'

'Pat Hobby,' he said. 'Can I wait here a minute? Man I came to see is at lunch.'

He sat down across from her and picked up a copy of a photo magazine.

'Oh, just let me mark that,' she said quickly.

He looked at the page which she checked. It showed paintings being boxed and carted away to safety from an art gallery in Europe.

'How'll you use it?' he said.

'Well, I thought it would be dramatic if there was an old man around while they were packing the pictures. A poor old man, trying to get a job helping them. But they can't

pushed it open: opened the door by pushing it
frail-looking: with a fragile look □ **sat:** to sit, sat, sat
he's left: he is no longer in; to leave, left, left
gave: to give, gave, given □ **forgot:** to forget, forgot, forgotten
put up: inscribe on the door
you a writer: are you a writer?
work at it: try to be one
ought to: should □ **get 'em to:** make them □ **test:** an acting test

what's that: what is that book

tip: piece of advice □ **the way to:** the best way to
get the guts: get the contents, get the most important part

I've been here: I have been in Hollywood

what stuck in their minds: what they particularly remember; to stick, stuck, stuck □ **write it down:** put it on paper

advice: opinion given to counsel

man I came to see: the man I came to see
across from her: opposite her □ **picked up:** took
photo magazine: magazine illustrated with photographs
mark that: make a note of
checked: was marking a note of
boxed: put in boxes □ **carted away to safety:** sent to safe places
art gallery: museum
how'll you use it?: how will you use it?
dramatic: impressive, striking
around: standing near □ **while:** *pendant que* □ **packing:** putting the pictures in boxes

use him — he's in the way — not even good cannon fodder. They want strong young people in the world. And it turns out he's the man who painted the pictures many years ago.'

Pat considered.

'It's good but I don't get it,' he said.

'Oh, it's nothing, a short short maybe.'

'Got any good picture ideas? I'm in with all the markets here.'

'I'm under contract.'

'Use another name.'

Her phone rang.

'Yes, this is Pricilla Smith,' the girl said.

After a minute she turned to Pat.

'Will you excuse me? This is a private call.'

He got it and walked out, and along the corridor. Finding an office with no name on it he went in and fell asleep on the couch.

II

Late that afternoon he returned to Jack Berners' waiting rooms. He had an idea about a man who meets a girl in an office and he thinks she's a stenographer but she turns out to be a writer. He engages her as a stenographer, though, and they start for the South Seas. It was a beginning, it was something to tell Jack, he thought — and, picturing Pricilla Smith, he refurbished some old business he hadn't seen used for years.

He became quite excited about it — felt quite young for a moment and walked up and down the waiting room

in the way: useless, a nuisance ☐ **even:** *même* ☐ **cannon fodder:** *chair à canon*
turns out: is revealed

considered: reflected, thought for a moment
I don't get it: I don't understand
short: short film or documentary shown with full-length picture
got: have you got ☐ **I'm in with:** I know ☐ **markets:** producers

I'm under contract: I have signed a contract

rang: to ring, rang, rung

turned to: she addressed herself to
private call: personal conversation
got it: understood ☐ **walked out:** went out
no name on it: no name on the door ☐ **went:** to go, went, gone
fell asleep: went to sleep ☐ **couch:** sofa

late: toward the end of the afternoon ☐ **waiting rooms:** where people who have appointments sit and wait
turns out: is found to be

though: however ☐ **start for:** leave for, go away to
thought: to think, thought, thought
picturing: imagining ☐ **refurbished:** renewed, tried to make new ☐ **business:** classic film scenes ☐ **used:** used in films
became : to become, became, become ☐ **quite:** very ☐ **felt:** to feel, felt, felt ☐ **walked up and down:** *fit les cent pas*

mentally rehearsing the first sequence. 'So here we have a situation like *It Happened One Night* — only *new*. I see Hedy Lamarr —'

Oh, he knew how to talk to these boys if he could get to them, with something to say.

'Mr. Berners still busy?' he asked for the fifth time.

'Oh, yes, Mr. Hobby. Mr. Bill Costello and Mr. Bach are in there.'

He thought quickly. It was half-past five. In the old days he had just busted in sometimes and sold an idea, an idea good for a couple of grand because it was just the moment when they were very tired of what they were doing at present.

He walked innocently out and to another door in the hall. He knew it led through a bathroom right in to Jack Berners' office. Drawing a quick breath he plunged...

'... So that's the notion,' he concluded after five minutes. 'It's just a flash — nothing really worked out, but you could give me an office and a girl and I could have something on paper for you in three days.'

Berners, Costello and Bach did not even have to look at each other. Berners spoke for them all as he said firmly and gently:

'That's no idea, Pat. I can't put you on salary for that.'

'Why don't you work it out further by yourself,' suggested Bill Costello. 'And then let's see it. We're looking for ideas — especially about the war.'

'A man can think better on salary,' said Pat.

There was silence. Costello and Bach had drunk with him, played poker with him, gone to the races with him. They'd honestly be glad to see him placed.

rehearsing: practicing □ **sequence:** scene
***It Happened One Night*:** film by Frank Capra (1934) with Clark Gable and Claudette Colbert □ **Hedy Lamarr:** Hollywood star of the 30s and 40s □ **these boys:** producers □ **get to:** get access to

still: *encore* □ **busy:** occupied

in the old days: in the past
busted in: come in without an appointment □ **sold:** to sell, sold, sold
good for: that they would pay for □ **a couple of grand:** 2,000 dollars

led: went; to lead, led, led □ **right:** just
drawing a quick breath: breathing as if about to plunge
notion: idea
flash: outline of the story □ **worked out:** developed, elaborated
girl: secretary
on paper: written out, ready
look at each other: *se regarder*
spoke: to speak, spoke, spoken □ **as:** when
gently: kindly
no idea: not an idea □ **put you on salary:** employ you

work it out further: work on it a little more
then let's see it: then we will read it □ **we're looking for:** we want to find
on salary: with a salary
drunk: to drink, drank, drunk
gone: to go, went, gone □ **races:** horse-races
they'd: they would □ **glad:** happy □ **placed:** with a job

'The war, eh,' he said gloomily. 'Everything is war now, no matter how many credits a man has. Do you know what it makes me think of? It makes me think of a well-known painter in the discard. It's war time and he's useless — just a man in the way.' He warmed to his conception of himself, '— but all the time they're carting away *his own paintings* as the most valuable thing worth saving. And they won't even let me help. That's what it reminds me of.'

There was again silence for a moment.

'That isn't a bad idea,' said Bach thoughtfully. He turned to the others. 'You know? In itself?'

Bill Costello nodded.

'Not bad at all. And I know where we could spot it. Right at the end of the fourth sequence. We just change old Ames to a painter.'

Presently they talked money.

'I'll give you two weeks on it,' said Berners to Pat. 'At two-fifty.'

'Two-fifty!' objected Pat. 'Say there was one time you paid me ten times that!'

'That was ten years ago,' Jack reminded him. 'Sorry. Best we can do now.'

'You make me feel like that old painter —'

'Don't oversell it,' said Jack, rising and smiling. 'You're on the payroll.'

Pat went out with a quick step and confidence in his eyes. Half a grand — that would take the pressure off for a month and you could often stretch two weeks into three — sometimes four. He left the studio proudly through the front entrance, stopping at the liquor store for a half-pint to take back to his room.

gloomily: depressed
no matter how many... has: the number of credits is not considered important any more
well-known: famous □ **in the discard:** unwanted
in the way: a nuisance □ **warmed to:** became very interested in
his conception: his vision □ **carting away:** carried away
as: because they are □ **valuable:** precious
worth saving: precious enough to be saved □ **won't:** will not
reminds: makes me think

thoughtfully: pensively
in itself: *en soi*
nodded: inclined his head in assent
spot: put
right: just
Ames: a character in the film
presently: soon □ **talked money:** discussed the salary
two weeks on it: two weeks' salary to work on it
two-fifty: 250 dollars
objected: expressed disapproval □ **say:** *dites* □ **there was one time:** in the past □ **that:** the 250 dollars

best: it is the best

oversell it: exaggerate □ **rising:** standing up
on the payroll: employed, hired
with a quick step: walking quickly □ **confidence:** assurance
half a grand: 500 dollars □ **take the pressure off:** make things easier financially □ **stretch:** extend
left: went out; to leave, left, left □ **proudly:** very gratified
liquor: wines and spirits □ **half-pint:** quarter of a litre

By seven o'clock things were even better. Santa Anita tomorrow, if he could get an advance. And tonight — something festive ought to be done tonight. With a sudden rush of pleasure he went down to the phone in the lower hall, called the studio and asked for Miss Pricilla Smith's number. He hadn't met anyone so pretty for years...

In her apartment Pricilla Smith spoke rather firmly into the phone.

'I'm awfully sorry,' she said, 'but I couldn't possibly... No — and I'm tied up all the rest of the week.'

As she hung up, Jack Berners spoke from the couch.

'Who was it?'

'Oh, some man who came in the office,' she laughed, 'and told me never to read the story I was working on.'

'Shall I believe you?'

'You certainly shall. I'll even think of his name in a minute. But first I want to tell you about an idea I had this morning. I was looking at a photo in a magazine where they were packing up some works of art in the Tate Gallery in London. And I thought —'

by: at □ **Santa Anita:** horse races
advance: advance on his salary □ **tonight:** that night
something festive: some celebration □ **ought to:** should
rush: feeling
lower hall: the hall downstairs □ **called:** telephoned
hadn't met anyone: met no other girl; to meet, met, met

spoke: to speak, spoke, spoken □ **rather:** very

awfully: terribly
tied up: busy
hung up: put down the phone; to hang, hung, hung

told: to tell, told, told
shall I believe you: do you expect me to believe you
think of: remember

packing up: putting in boxes
thought: to think, thought, thought

Grammaire au fil des nouvelles

En traduisant les phrases suivantes au moyen des structures suggérées en italiques entre parenthèses essayez de retrouver le texte anglais dont la page et la ligne sont indiquées par des chiffres : le premier renvoie à la page, le second à la ligne.

Cela faisait quinze ans qu'il y travaillait (*temps du passé,* 14.2).

Il pouvait toujours entrer en téléphonant à Lou (*expression du moyen ; gérondif,* 14.5).

Il n'avait jamais écrit beaucoup (*plus-que-parfait ; place de l'adverbe de temps,* 14.7).

On ne peut engager quelqu'un s'il n'a pas une idée de scénario (*traduction de à moins que,* 14.23).

La guerre venait d'éclater (*temps du passé,* 16.3).

Si tu arrives à persuader l'un d'eux de s'intéresser à ton sujet, amène-le moi (*structure "causative" ; construction de s'intéresser à,* 16.16).

Cela faisait vingt ans qu'il était dans la partie (*temps du passé ; expression de la durée,* 16.29).

Une fille à l'air fragile était assise et lisait un livre (*adjectifs composés ; forme en* **-ing**, 18.2).

Voilà un conseil très original (*substantifs indénombrables,* 18.20).

La photo montrait des tableaux qu'on mettait dans des caisses (*forme en* **-ing** *et passif,* 18.31).

Vous savez à quoi cela me fait penser ? Cela me fait penser à un vieux peintre oublié (*traduction de faire + verbe,* 24.3).

C'est cela que la situation me rappelle (*traduction de se rappeler,* 24.9).

Cela faisait des années qu'il n'avait pas rencontré une fille aussi jolie (*temps du passé,* 26.7).

‘BOIL SOME WATER — LOTS OF IT’

Pat Hobby sat in his office in the writer's building and looked at his morning's work, just come back from the script department. He was on a 'polish job', about the only kind he ever got nowadays. He was to repair a messy sequence in a hurry, but the word 'hurry' neither frightened nor inspired him for Pat had been in Hollywood since he was thirty — now he was forty-nine. All the work he had done this morning (except a little changing around of lines so he could claim them as his own) — all he had actually invented was a single imperative sentence, spoken by a doctor.

'Boil some water — lots of it.'

It was a good line. It had sprung into his mind full grown as soon as he had read the script. In the old silent days Pat would have used it as a spoken title and ended his dialogue worries for a space, but he needed some spoken words for other people in the scene. Nothing came.

'Boil some water', he repeated to himself. 'Lots of it.'

The word boil brought a quick glad thought of the commissary. A reverent thought too — for an old-timer like Pat, what people you sat with at lunch was more important in getting along than what you dictated in your office. This was no art, as he often said — this was an industry.

'This is no art,' he remarked to Max Leam who was leisurely drinking at a corridor water cooler. 'This is an industry.'

Max had flung him this timely bone of three weeks at three-fifty.

'Say look, Pat! Have you got anything down on paper yet?'

'Say I've got some stuff already that'll make 'em —' He

writer: scriptwriter
his morning's work: what he had written in the morning
on: working on ☐ **'polish job':** rewriting job
kind: sort ☐ **nowadays:** now ☐ **was to:** had to ☐ **messy:** incoherent
in a hurry: quickly ☐ **frightened:** alarmed
neither...nor: *ni...ni* ☐ **for:** because

lines: lines of dialogue
claim: pretend ☐ **his own:** his personal work ☐ **actually:** in fact
single: unique

sprung: appeared suddenly; to spring, sprang, sprung ☐ **full grown:** complete ☐ **silent days:** the days of silent films
spoken title: text flashed on the screen ☐ **ended:** solved
worries: problems ☐ **for a space:** for a time ☐ **needed:** required
came: to come, came, come

brought a quick glad thought: made him think with pleasure
commissary: cafeteria ☐ **reverent:** respectful ☐ **old-timer:** veteran
what people: the sort of people ☐ **sat:** to sit, sat, sat
getting along: advancing your career
no art: not art

leisurely: taking his time ☐ **water cooler:** dispenser of cold drinking water
flung: gave; one flings a bone at a dog ☐ **timely:** opportune
three-fifty: 350 dollars a week
say look: *dis voir* ☐ **down on paper:** written
yet: already
stuff: material, lines ☐ **'em:** them

named a familiar biological function with the somewhat startling assurance that it would take place in the theatre.

Max tried to gauge his sincerity.

'Want to read it to me now?' he asked.

'Not yet. But it's got the old guts if you know what I mean.'

Max was full of doubts.

'Well, go to it. And if you run into any medical snags check with the doctor over at the First Aid Station. It's got to be right.'

The spirit of Pasteur shone firmly in Pat's eyes.

'It will be.'

He felt good walking across the lot with Max — so good that he decided to glue himself to the producer and sit down with him at the Big Table. But Max foiled his intention by cooing 'See you later' and slipping into the barber shop.

Once Pat had been a familiar figure at the Big Table; often in his golden prime he had dined in the private canteens of executives. Being of the older Hollywood he understood their jokes, their vanities, their social system with its swift fluctuations. But there were too many new faces at the Big Table now — faces that looked at him with the universal Hollywood suspicion. And at the little tables where the young writers sat they seemed to take work so seriously. As for just sitting down anywhere, even with secretaries or extras — Pat would rather catch a sandwich at the corner.

Detouring to the Red Cross Station he asked for the doctor. A girl, a nurse, answered from a wall mirror where she was hastily drawing her lips, 'He's out. What is it?'

'Oh. Then I'll come back.'

somewhat: a little, rather
startling: surprising
tried: cf. to try □ **to gauge:** to measure, to estimate
want...: do you want...
it's got: it has got □ **guts:** intensity, force

was full of doubts: did not believe him
go to it: go on working □ **run into:** meet □ **snags:** problems
check: test, verify □ **First Aid Station:** infirmary
it's got to: it must
shone...in Pat's eyes: illuminated Pat's eyes

the lot: the studio
glue himself: follow □ **producer:** who produces films
Big Table: reserved for important people □ **foiled:** frustrated
cooing: murmuring □ **later:** another time □ **slipping:** escaping

once: in the past
his golden prime: when he was successful
executives: producers □ **older Hollywood:** the Hollywood of the past □ **jokes:** pleasantries □ **swift:** quick
new faces: new people
universal: usual, common
suspicion: distrust, scepticism
sat: to sit, sat, sat □ **seemed:** appeared
as for: *quant à* □ **anywhere:** at any table
extras: *figurants* □ **would rather:** preferred to □ **catch:** eat
corner: at the corner shop
detouring: making a detour
nurse: woman taking care of the sick □ **wall mirror:** mirror hanging on the wall □ **drawing her lips:** putting lipstick on her lips

She had finished, and now she turned — vivid and young and with a bright consoling smile.

'Miss Stacey will help you. I'm about to go to lunch.'

He was aware of an old, old feeling — left over from the time when he had had wives — a feeling that to invite this little beauty to lunch might cause trouble. But he remembered quickly that he didn't have any wives now — they had both given up asking for alimony.

'I'm working on a medical,' he said. 'I need some help.'

'A medical?'

'Writing it — idea about a doc. Listen — let me buy you lunch. I want to ask you some medical questions.'

The nurse hesitated.

'I don't know. It's my first day out here.'

'It's all right,' he assured her, 'studios are democratic; everybody is just "Joe" or "Mary" — from the big shots right down to the prop boys.'

He proved it magnificently on their way to lunch by greeting a male star and getting his own name back in return. And in the commissary, where they were placed hard by the Big Table, his producer, Max Leam, looked up, did a little 'takem' and winked.

The nurse — her name was Helen Earle — peered about eagerly.

'I don't see anybody,' she said. 'Except oh, there's Ronald Colman. I didn't know Ronald Colman looked like that.'

Pat pointed suddenly to the floor.

'And there's Mickey Mouse!'

She jumped and Pat laughed at his joke — but Helen Earle was already staring starry-eyed at the costume extras

vivid: full of life, energetic
bright: cheerful, happy
I'm about: I'm going to
aware: conscious □ **feeling:** sensation □ **left over:** surviving
...wives: Pat has been married several times; cf. a wife

given up: stopped; to give up + V...ing □ **alimony:** *pension alimentaire* □ **a medical:** a film set in the medical world

idea about: I've got an idea bout □ **doc:** doctor □ **buy you lunch:** invite you to lunch

my first day out here: my first day in this office

big shots: important people, executives and producers
right down: all the way down □ **prop:** stage property, accessories

by greeting: by saying 'Hello' to □ **getting:** receiving
commissary: cafeteria
hard by: close to □ **looked up:** raised his head
did a little 'takem': showed some surprise □ **winked:** closed and opened one eye very quickly □ **peered about:** looked closely around her at her neighbours □ **eagerly:** much interested

Ronald Colman: (1891-1958) romantic British actor

pointed: pointed his finger

she jumped: she jumped out of fear
staring: looking fixedly □ **starry-eyed:** full of admiration

who filled the hall with the colors of the First Empire. Pat was piqued to see her interest go out to these nonentities.

'The big shots are at this next table,' he said solemnly, wistfully, 'directors and all except the biggest executives. They could have Ronald Colman pressing pants. I usually sit over there but they don't want ladies. At lunch, that is, they don't want ladies.'

'Oh,' said Helen Earle, polite but unimpressed. 'It must be wonderful to be a writer too. It's so very interesting.'

'It has its points,' he said... he had thought for years it was a dog's life.

'What is it you want to ask me about a doctor?'

Here was toil again. Something in Pat's mind snapped off when he thought of the story.

'Well, Max Leam — that man facing us — Max Leam and I have a script about a Doc. You know? Like a hospital picture?'

'I know.' And she added after a moment, 'That's the reason that I went in training.'

'And we've got to have it *right* because a hundred million people would check on it. So this doctor in the script he tells them to boil some water. He says, "Boil some water — lots of it." And we were wondering what the people would do then.'

'Why — they'd probably boil it,' Helen said, and then, somewhat confused by the question, 'What people?'

'Well, somebody's daughter and the man that lived there and an attorney and the man that was hurt.'

Helen tried to digest this before answering.

'— and some other guy I'm going to cut out,' he finished.

First Empire: Napoleonic empire
piqued: offended □ **nonentities:** unimportant people
big shots: important people □ **next:** nearby
wistfully: with nostalgia □ **all except:** everything except
pressing pants: working at a cleaner's
over there: at the Big Table
that is: that is to say
unimpressed: indifferent
so very: extremely

points: advantages □ **thought:** to think, thought, thought
a dog's life: a life of misery

toil: hard work □ **snapped off:** broke, disconnected itself

facing us: in front of us
script: scenario □ **doc:** doctor □ **like:** something like

went in training: became a nurse
we've got to have it right: we musn't make mistakes
check: verify

we were wondering: we wanted to know
then: in this situation
why: well
somewhat: a little □ **confused:** perplexed
somebody: one character in the scenario
attorney: lawyer □ **that was hurt:** that had had an accident
tried: cf. to try □ **digest:** understand
some other guy: another man □ **cut out:** of the scenario

There was a pause. The waitress set down tuna fish sandwiches.

'Well, when a doctor gives orders they're orders,' Helen decided.

'Hm.' Pat's interest had wandered to an odd little scene at the Big Table while he inquired absently, 'You married?'

'No.'

'Neither am I.'

Beside the Big Table stood an extra. A Russian Cossack with a fierce moustache. He stood resting his hand on the back of an empty chair between Director Paterson and Producer Leam.

'Is this taken?' he asked, with a thick Central European accent.

All along the Big Table faces stared suddenly at him. Until after the first look the supposition was that he must be some well-known actor. But he was not — he was dressed in one of the many-colored uniforms that dotted the room.

Someone at the table said: 'That's taken.' But the man drew out the chair and sat down.

'Got to eat somewhere,' he remarked with a grin.

A shiver went over the near-by tables. Pat Hobby stared with his mouth ajar. It was as if someone had crayoned Donald Duck into the *Last Supper*.

'Look at that,' he advised Helen. 'What they'll do to him! Boy!'

The flabbergasted silence at the Big Table was broken by Ned Harman, the Production Manager.

'This table is reserved,' he said.

The extra looked up from a menu.

waitress: girl serving customers ☐ **set down:** brought ☐ **tuna fish:** *thon*
they're: they are

wandered to: been distracted by ☐ **odd:** strange
inquired: asked ☐ **absently:** without interest ☐ **you married:** are you married

neither am I: I am not married either
beside: near ☐ **stood:** was standing ☐ **Cossack:** *Cosaque*
fierce: aggressive, bellicose ☐ **resting his hand:** with his hand
back: *dossier* ☐ **empty:** unoccupied ☐ **director:** who directs films
producer: who produces films
taken: occupied ☐ **thick:** marked

all along: all round ☐ **stared:** looked fixedly
until after the first look: before looking at him
well-known: famous
dressed in: wearing ☐ **dotted:** could be seen here and there

that's: that chair is
drew out: pulled out ☐ **sat:** to sit, sat, sat
got to eat somewhere: I must eat somewhere ☐ **grin:** ironical smile
shiver: *frisson* ☐ **near-by:** near the Big Table
ajar: open
crayoned: drawn a picture of ☐ **Last Supper:** famous painting by Leonardo Da Vinci ☐ **advised:** recommended
boy: my God
flabbergasted: shocked ☐ **broken:** interrupted; to break, broke, broken

looked up: raised his head

'They told me sit anywhere.'

He beckoned a waitress — who hesitated, looking for an answer in the faces of her superiors.

'Extras don't eat here,' said Max Leam, still politely. 'This is a —'

'I got to eat,' said the Cossack doggedly. 'I've been standing around six hours while they shoot this stinking mess and now I got to eat.'

The silence had extended — from Pat's angle all within range seemed to be poised in mid-air.

The extra shook his head wearily.

'I dunno who cooked it up —' he said — and Max Leam sat forward in his chair — 'but it's the lousiest tripe I ever seen shot in Hollywood.'

— At his table Pat was thinking why didn't they do something? Knock him down, drag him away. If they were yellow themselves they could call the studio police.

'Who is that?' Helen Earle was following his eyes innocently. 'Somebody I ought to know?'

He was listening attentively to Max Leam's voice, raised in anger.

'Get up and get out of here, buddy, and get out quick!'

The extra frowned.

'Who's telling me?' he demanded.

'You'll see.' Max appealed to the table at large, 'Where's Cushman — where's the Personnel man?'

'You try to move me,' said the extra, lifting the hilt of his scabbard above the level of the table, 'and I'll hang this on your ear. I know my rights.'

The dozen men at the table, representing a thousand dollars an hour in salaries, sat stunned. Far down by the door one of the studio police caught wind of what was

anywhere: at any table
beckoned: made a sign to □ **looking for:** waiting for
her superiors: the important people at the Big Table
still politely: as politely as before

I got to eat: I've got to eat □ **doggedly:** with obstination
standing around: waiting □ **shoot:** film □ **stinking mess:** nasty, unpleasant film
from Pat's angle: from what Pat could see □ **within range:** sitting near-by □ **poised in mid-air:** frozen, paralysed
shook: moved □ **wearily:** with lassitude
dunno: don't know □ **cooked it up:** wrote it, arranged it
sat forward: sat up □ **lousiest tripe:** most stupid nonsense
I ever seen: I have ever seen □ **shot:** filmed

knock him down: strike him □ **drag him away:** take him away by force □ **yellow:** afraid, cowardly
following his eyes: looking in the same direction
somebody I ought to know: a famous person everybody knows
raised: loud

get up: leave the table □ **buddy:** friend
frowned: *fronça le sourcil*
who's telling me: who's telling me to go
appealed to...at large: addressed himself to the entire table
the Personnel man: the man responsible for personnel
lifting: raising up □ **hilt:** handle
scabbard: *fourreau* □ **above:** higher than □ **hang:** suspend

the dozen men: the twelve men
stunned: paralysed □ **far down:** at some distance □ **by the door:** near the door □ **caught wind:** remarked, saw, noticed

happening and started to elbow through the crowded room. And Big Jack Wilson, another director, was on his feet in an instant coming around the table.

But they were too late — Pat Hobby could stand no more. He had jumped up, seizing a big heavy tray from the serving stand nearby. In two springs he reached the scene of action — lifting the tray he brought it down upon the extra's head with all the strength of his forty-nine years. The extra, who had been in the act of rising to meet Wilson's threatened assault, got the blow full on his face and temple and as he collapsed a dozen red streaks sprang into sight through the heavy grease paint. He crashed sideways between the chairs.

Pat stood over him panting — the tray in his hand.

'The dirty rat!' he cried. 'Where does he think —'

The studio policeman pushed past; Wilson pushed past — the two aghast men from another table rushed up to survey the situation.

'It was a gag!' one of them shouted. 'That's Walter Herrick, the writer. It's his picture.'

'My God!'

'He was kidding Max Leam. It was a gag I tell you!'

'Pull him out... Get a doctor... Look out, there!'

Now Helen Earle hurried over; Walter Herrick was dragged out into a cleared space on the floor and there were yells of 'Who did it? — Who beaned him?'

Pat let the tray lapse to a chair, its sound unnoticed in the confusion.

He saw Helen Earle working swiftly at the man's head with a pile of clean napkins.

'Why did they have to do this to him?' someone shouted.

elbow through: make their way ☐ **crowded:** full of people
was on his feet: stood up
coming round the table: and he was coming round the table
could stand no more: couldn't endure the situation anymore
jumped up: stood up quickly ☐ **seized:** took ☐ **tray:** *plateau*
stand: table for plates, dishes ☐ **springs:** bounds ☐ **reached:** arrived at ☐ **lifting:** raising high ☐ **brought it down:** banged it
strength: energy; cf. strong
in the act of: just ☐ **to meet:** to face
threatened assault: menace ☐ **got:** received ☐ **full on:** in the middle of ☐ **collapsed:** fell down ☐ **red streaks:** traces of blood ☐ **sprang... paint:** suddenly appeared under his thick make-up ☐ **crashed sideways:** fell on his side
over him: above him ☐ **panting:** breathing quickly
dirty rat: bastard, devil ☐ **cried:** exclaimed
pushed past: arrived on the scene
aghast: frozen, petrified ☐ **rushed up:** came running
survey: observe
gag: joke ☐ **shouted:** exclaimed loudly
picture: film

kidding: making fun of
look out: be careful
hurried over: came quickly to the scene
dragged out: pulled out, taken out ☐ **cleared:** empty
yells: angry shouts ☐ **beaned him:** hit him on the head
lapse: fall ☐ **its sound unnoticed:** no one heard the sound

swiftly: quickly ☐ **at the man's head:** on the man's face
napkins: servietes
why did they have to do this: why must they do this

Pat caught Max Leam's eye but Max happened to look away at the moment and a sense of injustice came over Pat. He alone in this crisis, real or imaginary, had *acted.* He alone had played the man, while those stuffed shirts let themselves be insulted and abused. And now he would have to take the rap — because Walter Herrick was powerful and popular, a three thousand a week man who wrote hit shows in New York. How could anyone have guessed that it was a gag?

There was a doctor now. Pat saw him say something to the manageress and her shrill voice sent the waitresses scattering like leaves toward the kitchen.

'Boil some water! Lots of it!'

The words fell wild and unreal on Pat's burdened soul. But even though he now knew at first hand what came next, he did not think that he could go on from there.

caught...eye: tried to attract his attention ☐ **happened to look away:** looked away as if by chance ☐ **came over:** invaded
he alone: he was the only one who
while: *tandis que* ☐ **stuffed shirts:** pompous people
let themselves: suffered themselves to ☐ **abused:** humiliated
take the rap: take the blame, be criticized
powerful: influential ☐ **a three thousand a week man:** a man who earned 3,000 dollars a week ☐ **hit:** popular, successful
guessed: divined

manageress: female boss ☐ **shrill:** high, piercing ☐ **sent... leaves:** caused all the waitresses to run ☐ **toward:** in the direction of

fell: sounded, felt ☐ **wild:** strange ☐ **burdened:** oppressed
soul: spirit ☐ **even though:** even if ☐ **at first hand:** from direct experience ☐ **next:** after that ☐ **go on from there:** use this in his script

Grammaire au fil des nouvelles

En traduisant les phrases suivantes au moyen des structures suggérées en italiques entre parenthèses essayez de retrouver le texte anglais dont la page et la ligne sont indiquées par des chiffres : le premier renvoie à la page, le second à la ligne.

Le bâtiment des scénaristes...son travail de la matinée...le service des scénarios... (*génitif et noms composés,* 30.1,2,3).

Il était censé arranger en vitesse une scène mal ficelée (*traduction de devoir,* 30.4).

Les gens avec lesquels on déjeune, c'est plus important que ce que l'on dicte dans son bureau (*proposition relative,* 30.21).

Il faut que ce soit véridique (*traduction de devoir,* 32.10).

Il y avait trop de nouveaux visages autour de la Grande Table (*quantifieurs,* 32.21).

Pat préférait manger un sandwich au coin (*construction de* **'d rather**, 32.26).

Vous êtes mariée? — Non. — Moi non plus (*reprise de l'auxiliaire,* 38.9).

C'est le navet le plus minable que j'aie jamais vu tourner à Hollywood (*superlatif ; traduction de jamais,* 40.13).

Les figurants ne peuvent pas manger ici (*détermination,* 40.4).

Qui est-ce ? Quelqu'un que je devrais connaître ? (*traduction de devoir,* 40.19).

Pat laissa le plateau glisser par terre (*traduction de laisser,* 42.27).

TEAMED WITH GENIUS

"I took a chance in sending for you", said Jack Berners. "But there's a job that you just *may* be able to help out with."

Though Pat Hobby was not offended, either as man or writer, a formal protest was called for.

"I been in the industry fifteen years, Jack. I've got more screen credits than a dog has got fleas."

"Maybe I chose the wrong word", said Jack. "What I mean is, that was a long time ago. About money we'll pay you just what Republic paid you last month — three-fifty a week. Now — did you ever hear of a writer named René Wilcox?"

The name was unfamiliar. Pat had scarcely opened a book in a decade.

"She's pretty good", he ventured.

"It's a man, an English playwright. He's only here in L.A. for his health. Well — we've had a Russian Ballet picture kicking around for a year — three bad scripts on it. So last week we signed up René Wilcox — he seemed just the person."

Pat considered.

"You mean he's —"

"I don't know and I don't care", interrupted Berners sharply. "We think we can borrow Zorina, so we want to hurry things up — do a shooting script instead of just a treatment. Wilcox is inexperienced and that's where you come in. You used to be a good man for structure."

"*Used* to be!"

"All right, maybe you still are." Jack beamed with momentary encouragement. "Find yourself an office and get together with René Wilcox." As Pat started out he called him back and put a bill in his hand. "First of all,

chance: risk ☐ **sending for:** calling
just: possibly
help out: help
offended: hurt ☐ **either... or:** soit... soit
called for: necessary, required
I been: I have been ☐ **industry:** film business ☐ **I've got... screen credits:** I have written more films ☐ **fleas:** *puces*
chose: cf. to choose

Republic: Republic Studios ☐ **three-fifty:** 350 dollars
hear of: hear someone talk of

unfamiliar: unknown to him ☐ **scarcely:** pratically never
decade: period of ten years
pretty: very ☐ **ventured:** took the risk of saying
playwright: who writes plays for the theatre
L.A.: Los Angeles ☐ **health:** condition of the body
kicking around: being discussed without any results
signed up: hired
just the person: the right person
considered: thought for a moment

sharply: abruptly ☐ **borrow:** get temporary use of
hurry... up: accelerate ☐ **shooting script:** scenario
treatment: synopsis
come in: play your part ☐ **used to be:** were in the past

beamed: smiled

get together: get to meet ☐ **started out:** started to go out
bill: some money

get a new hat. You used to be quite a boy around the secretaries in the old days. Don't give up at forty-nine!"

Over in the Writer's Building Pat glanced at the directory in the hall and knocked at the door of 216. No answer, but he went in to discover a blond, willowy youth of twenty-five staring moodily out the window.

"Hello, René!" Pat said. "I'm your partner."

Wilcox's regard questioned even his existence, but Pat continued heartily, "I hear we're going to lick some stuff into shape. Ever collaborate before?"

"I have never written for the cinema before."

While this increased Pat's chance for a screen credit he badly needed, it meant that he might have to do some work. The very thought made him thirsty.

"This is different from playwriting", he suggested, with suitable gravity.

"Yes — I read a book about it."

Pat wanted to laugh. In 1928 he and another man had concocted such a sucker-trap, *Secrets of Film Writing*. It would have made money if pictures hadn't started to talk.

"It all seems simple enough", said Wilcox. Suddenly he took his hat from the rack. "I'll be running along now."

"Don't you want to talk about the script?" demanded Pat. "What have you done so far?"

"I've not done anything", said Wilcox deliberately. "That idiot, Berners, gave me some trash and told me to go on from there. But it's too dismal." His blue eyes narrowed. "I say, what's a boom shot?"

"A boom shot? Why, that's when the camera's on a crane."

Pat leaned over the desk and picked up a blue-jacketed "Treatment." On the cover he read:

quite a boy: very successful ☐ **around:** with
in the old days: in the past ☐ **give up:** stop
glanced: looked briefly ☐ **directory:** list of offices

went in: entered ☐ **willowy:** *mince* ☐ **youth:** *jeune homme*
staring: looking fixedly ☐ **moodily:** sadly

regard: look ☐ **questioned:** doubted
heartily: with enthusiasm ☐ **stuff:** material
lick... into shape: work on ☐ **ever:** *jamais*

while: though ☐ **increased:** augmented
badly: very much ☐ **needed:** cf. to need ☐ **meant:** cf. to mean
the very thought: the thought itself ☐ **made him thirsty:** made him want a drink
suitable: appropriate

concocted: produced ☐ **sucker-trap:** a book designed for idiots
made money: been profitable ☐ **talk:** use sound

rack: shelf or shelves ☐ **running along:** leaving, going out

so far: up to now, until now
deliberately: slowly, cautiously
trash: nonsense, rubbish
dismal: sad, depressing
his eyes narrowed: he half closed his eyes ☐ **boom shot:** *travelling vertical* ☐ **that's:** that is ☐ **camera's:** camera is
crane: *grue*
leaned: inclined his body ☐ **picked up:** took ☐ **blue-jacketed:** with a blue cover

BALLET SHOES

A Treatment

by

Consuela Martin

An Original from an idea by Consuela Martin

Pat glanced at the beginning and then at the end.

"I'd like it better if we could get the war in somewhere", he said frowning. "Have the dancer go as a Red Cross nurse and then she could get regenerated. See what I mean?"

There was no answer. Pat turned and saw the door softly closing.

What is this? he exclaimed. What kind of collaborating can a man do if he walks out? Wilcox had not even given the legitimate excuse — the races at Santa Anita!

The door opened again, a pretty girl's face, rather frightened, showed itself momentarily, said "Oh", and disappeared. Then it returned.

"Why it's Mr. Hobby!" she exclaimed. "I was looking for Mr. Wilcox."

He fumbled for her name but she supplied it.

"Katherine Hodge. I was your secretary when I worked here three years ago."

Pat knew she had once worked with him, but for the moment could not remember whether there had been a deeper relation. It did not seem to him that it had been love — but looking at her now, that appeared rather too bad.

"Sit down", said Pat. "You assigned to Wilcox?"

"I thought so — but he hasn't given me any work yet."

original: first version

glanced: looked □ **then:** after that
get the war in: introduce scenes about the war
frowning: *fronçant les sourcils* □ **have the dancer:** make the dancer
nurse: *infirmière*

saw: cf. to see
softly: without any noise
collaborating: collaboration

legitimate: acceptable, usual □ **races:** horse races

frightened: afraid □ **momentarily:** for a moment

looking for: trying to find

fumbled: tried to find □ **supplied:** gave

once: at one time
whether: if
deeper: more intimate □ **seem:** appear
rather too bad: really a pity

you assigned: have you been assigned □ **assigned:** alloted

"I think he's nuts", Pat said gloomily. "He asked me what a boom shot was. Maybe he's sick — that's why he's out here. He'll probably start throwing up all over the office."

"He's well now", Katherine ventured.

"He doesn't look like it to me. Come on in my office. You can work for *me* this afternoon."

Pat lay on his couch while Miss Katherine Hodge read the script of *Ballet Shoes* aloud to him. About midway in the second sequence he fell asleep with his new hat on his chest.

Except for the hat, that was the identical position in which he found René next day at eleven. And it was that way for three straight days — one was asleep or else the other — and sometimes both. On the fourth day they had several conferences in which Pat again put forward his idea about the war as a regenerating force for ballet dancers.

"Couldn't we *not* talk about the war?" suggested René. "I have two brothers in the Guards."

"You're lucky to be here in Hollywood."

"That's as it may be."

"Well, what's your idea of the start of the picture?"

"I do not like the present beginning. It gives me an almost physical nausea."

"So then, we got to have something in its place. That's why I want to plant the war —"

"I'm late to luncheon," said René Wilcox. "Good-bye, Mike."

Pat grumbled to Katherine Hodge:

"He can call me anything he likes, but somebody's got

nuts: crazy, mad ☐ **gloomily:** sadly
sick: ill, not well
out here: over here in Los Angeles ☐ **throwing up:** *vomir*

well: in good health ☐ **ventured:** said timidly
look like it: appear well

lay: was lying on his bed; to lie ☐ **couch:** sofa
aloud: loudly; cf. a loud voice ☐ **midway:** half way
sequence: scene
chest: *poitrine*

for the hat: that he had no hat
next day: the day after ☐ **that way:** like this
straight: consecutive
both: the two of them ☐ **fourth:** 4th
put forward: proposed
regenerating: purifying

couldn't we not talk: could we stop talking

that's as it may be: that is possible
start: beginning

we got to: we must
plant: introduce
luncheon: lunch

grumbled: complained
anything: any name

to write this picture. I'd go to Jack Berners and tell him — but I think we'd both be out on our ears."

For two days more he camped in René's office, trying to rouse him to action, but with no avail. Desperate on the following day — when the playwright did not even come to the studio — Pat took a benzedrine tablet and attacked the story alone. Pacing his office with the treatment in his hand he dictated to Katherine — interspersing the dictation with a short, biased history of his life in Hollywood. At the day's end he had two pages of script.

The ensuing week was the toughest in his life — not even a moment to make a pass at Katherine Hodge. Gradually with many creaks, his battered hulk got in motion. Benzedrine and great drafts of coffee woke him in the morning, whiskey anesthetized him at night. Into his feet crept an old neuritis and as his nerves began to crackle he developed a hatred against René Wilcox, which served him as a sort of *ersatz* fuel. He was going to finish the script by himself and hand it to Berners with the statement that Wilcox had not contributed a single line.

But it was too much — Pat was too far gone. He blew up when he was half through and went on a twenty-four-hour bat — and next morning arrived back at the studio to find a message that Mr. Berners wanted to see the script at four. Pat was in a sick and confused state when his door opened and René Wilcox came in with a typescript in one hand, and a copy of Berners' note in the other.

"It's all right", said Wilcox. "I've finished it."

"*What*? Have you been *working*?"

"I always work at night."

"What've you done? A treatment?"

"No, a shooting script. At first I was held back by

I'd go: I would go
we'd: we would ☐ **out on our ears:** sacked
trying: cf. to try
rouse him to action: stimulate him ☐ **with no avail:** in vain
following: next
benzedrine: drug used as stimulant ☐ **tablet:** small amount of drug
pacing: walking slowly ☐ **treatment:** synopsis
interspersing... with: stopping the dictation to give

the day's end: at the end of the day
ensuing: following, next ☐ **toughest:** hardest
make a pass: make advances to
creaks: difficulties ☐ **battered:** decrepit ☐ **hulk:** body
got in motion: started to work ☐ **drafts:** drinks ☐ **woke:** roused from sleep
crept: insinuated itself ☐ **neuritis:** pain ☐ **nerves:** nervous system
crackle: explode ☐ **hatred:** intense dislike
ersatz: substitute ☐ **fuel:** source of energy
by himself: alone, on his own ☐ **hand:** give
statement: declaration ☐ **not... a single:** not one
too far gone: already lost, hopeless ☐ **blew up:** exploded
was half through: had written one half of the script
he... went on a... bat: he spent the next twenty-four hours drinking

sick: not well, ill ☐ **state:** condition

what've: what have
shooting script: complete scenario ☐ **held back:** restrained, restricted

personal worries, but once I got started it was very simple. You just get behind the camera and dream."

Pat stood up aghast.

"But we were supposed to collaborate. Jack'll be wild."

"I've always worked alone", said Wilcox gently. "I'll explain to Berners this afternoon."

Pat sat in a daze. If Wilcox's script was good — but how could a first script be good? Wilcox should have fed it to him as he wrote; then they might have *had* something.

Fear started his mind working — he was struck by his first original idea since he had been on the job. He phoned to the script department for Katherine Hodge and when she came over told her what he wanted. Katherine hesitated.

"I just want to *read* it", Pat said hastily. "If Wilcox is there you can't take it, of course. But he just might be out."

He waited nervously. In five minutes she was back with the script.

"It isn't mimeographed or even bound", she said.

He was at the typewriter, trembling as he picked out a letter with two fingers.

"Can I help?" she asked.

"Find me a plain envelope and a used stamp and some paste."

Pat sealed the letter himself and then gave directions:

"Listen outside Wilcox's office. If he's in, push it under his door. If he's out get a call boy to deliver it to him, wherever he is. Say it's from the mail room. Then you better go off the lot for the afternoon. So he won't catch on, see?"

worries: problems ☐ **once:** after
get: put yourself ☐ **behind:** *derrière*
aghast: horrified
Jack'll be: Jack will be
wild: furious

in a daze: in a state of confusion
fed it to him: given it to him; cf. to feed
as: when
fear: alarm ☐ **started his mind working:** made him think
he was struck by: he thought of, he imagined

hastily: quickly
there: in his office

mimeographed: copied ☐ **bound:** between stiff covers; to bind
picked out: typed

plain: with nothing written on it ☐ **stamp :** *timbre*
paste: glue
sealed: closed ☐ **directions:** instructions
in: in his office ☐ **it:** the letter
call boy: messenger ☐ **deliver:** give
wherever: anywhere he might be ☐ **mail:** post
you better: you'd better ☐ **go off the lot:** leave the studio
catch on: understand what we are doing

As she went out Pat wished he had kept a copy of the note. He was proud of it — there was a ring of factual sincerity in it too often missing from his work.

"Dear Mr. Wilcox:

I am sorry to tell you your two brothers were killed in action today by a long range Tommy-gun. You are wanted at home in England right away.

John Smythe
The British Consulate, New York"

But Pat realized that this was no time for self-applause. He opened Wilcox's script.

To his vast surprise it was technically proficient — the dissolves, fades, cuts, pans and trucking shots were correctly detailed. This simplified everything. Turning back to the first page he wrote at the top:

BALLET SHOES

First Revise

From Pat Hobby and René Wilcox — presently changing this to read: *From René Wilcox and Pat Hobby.*

Then, working frantically, he made several dozen small changes. He substituted the word "Scram!" for "Get out of my sight!", he put "Behind the eight-ball" instead of "in trouble", and replaced "you'll be sorry" with the apt coinage "Or else!" Then he phoned the script department.

"This is Pat Hobby. I've been working on a script with René Wilcox, and Mr. Berners would like to have it mimeographed by half-past three."

wished he had kept: regretted he had not kept; to keep
proud of: very satisfied with ☐ **ring:** touch, tone ☐ **factual:** real, authentic ☐ **missing:** absent

in action: in battle
range: distance ☐ **Tommy-gun:** sub-machine gun
right away: immediately

no time: not the right time
self-applause: self-congratulation
vast: great ☐ **proficient:** showing expertise
dissolves... fades: *fondus enchaînés* ☐ **cuts:** *raccords* ☐ **pans:** panoramic effects ☐ **trucking shots:** *travelling vertical*

revise: version
presently: soon ☐ **this:** the order of the names

frantically: like a madman
scram: go away
eight-ball: term used in games of billiards; the eight-ball is the black ball ☐ **apt:** appropriate
coinage: expression ☐ **or else:** be careful

mimeographed: copied ☐ **by:** for, before

This would give him an hour's start on his unconscious collaborator.

"Is it an emergency?"

"I'll say."

"We'll have to split it up between several girls."

Pat continued to improve the script till the call boy arrived. He wanted to put in his war idea but time was short — still, he finally told the call boy to sit down, while he wrote laboriously in pencil on the last page.

CLOSE SHOT: *Boris and Rita*

Rita: *What does anything matter now! I have enlisted as a trained nurse in the war.*

Boris: (moved) *War purifies and regenerates!*

(He puts his arms around her in a wild embrace as the music soars way up and we FADE OUT)

Limp and exhausted by his effort he needed a drink, so he left the lot and slipped cautiously into the bar across from the studio where he ordered gin and water.

With the glow, he thought warm thoughts. He had done *almost* what he had been hired to do — though his hand had accidentally fallen upon the dialogue rather that the structure. But how could Berners tell that the structure wasn't Pat's? Katherine Hodge would say nothing, for fear of implicating herself. They were all guilty but guiltiest of all was René Wilcox for refusing to play the game. Always, according to his lights, Pat had played the game.

He had another drink, bought breath tablets and for a while amused himself at the nickel machine in the drugstore. Louie, the studio bookie, asked if he was

start: advantage □ **unconscious:** unknowing, unaware

an emergency: urgent work
I'll say: rather
split it up: divide it
improve: correct, make better □ **till:** until
put in: introduce
time was short: he didn't have enough time □ **still:** yet, but
laboriously: with difficulty

close shot: *plan rapproché*
what does anything matter: nothing is important □ **enlisted:** joined the Army □ **trained:** experienced
moved: with emotion
wild: unrestrained
soars: increases in volume □ **way up:** very high

limp: without energy □ **exhausted:** tired out
lot: studio □ **slipped:** went furtively □ **cautiously:** with prudence

glow: warmth induced by the gin □ **warm:** pleasant
almost: practically □ **hired:** employed
fallen upon: found
tell: discover, find out
Pat's: Pat's structure, written by Pat
for fear of: because she would be afraid of
guilty: criminal, culpable
play the game: work along traditional lines □ **according to his lights:** doing his best
breath tablets: to eliminate the smell of alcohol
while: moment □ **nickel:** *machine à sous*
bookie: bookmaker, who takes money from people to bet on horses

interested in wagers on a bigger scale.

"Not today, Louie."

"What are they paying you, Pat?"

"Thousand a week."

"Not so bad."

"Oh, a lot of us old-timers are coming back", Pat prophesied. "In silent days was where you got real training — with directors shooting off the cuff and needing a gag in a split second. Now it's a sis job. They got English teachers working in pictures! What do they know?"

"How about a little something on 'Quaker Girl'?"

"No", said Pat. "This afternoon I got an important angle to work on. I don't want to worry about horses."

At three-fifteen he returned to his office to find two copies of his script in bright new covers.

BALLET SHOES

from

René Wilcox and Pat Hobby

First Revise

It reassured him to see his name in type. As he waited in Jack Berners' anteroom he almost wished he had reversed the names. With the right director this might be another *It Happened One Night*, and if he got his name on something like that it meant a three or four year gravy ride. But this time he'd save his money — go to Santa Anita only once a week — get himself a girl along the type of Katherine Hodge, who wouldn't expect a mansion in Beverly Hills.

Berners' secretary interrupted his reverie, telling him to go in. As he entered he saw with gratification that a copy

wagers... scale: bigger bets

thousand: 1,000 dollars

old-timers: veterans
in silent days was where: it was when films were silent that
training: experience □ **shooting:** filming □ **off the cuff:** improvising
gag: joke □ **a split:** less than a □ **sis:** sissy effeminate, childish
what do they know: they know nothing about films

a little something: making a bet

angle: job

bright: in vivid colors

revise: revised version

in type: printed on the page
anteroom: waiting room □ **wished he had:** regretted he had not
right: correct, suitable
It Happened One Night: film by Frank Capra (1934) with Clark Gable and Claudette Colbert □ **gravy ride:** lucrative period
save: put it away safely, not spend it □ **Santa Anita:** Santa Anita horse races □ **girl:** girl-friend □ **along the tyne of:** like
expect: want to have □ **mansion:** luxurious residence

saw: cf. to see □ **gratification:** pleasure

of the new script lay on Berners' desk.

"Did you ever —" asked Berners suddenly "— go to a psychoanalyst?"

"No", admitted Pat. "But I suppose I could get up on it. Is it a new assignment?"

"Not exactly. It's just that I think you've lost your grip. Even larceny requires a certain cunning. I've just talked to Wilcox on the phone."

"Wilcox must be nuts", said Pat, aggressively. "I didn't steal anything from him. His name's on it, isn't it? Two weeks ago I laid out all his structure — every scene. I even wrote one whole scene — at the end about the war."

"Oh yes, the war", said Berners as if he was thinking of something else.

"But if you like Wilcox's ending better —"

"Yes, I like his ending better. I never saw a man pick up this work so fast." He paused. "Pat, you've told the truth just once since you came in this room — that you didn't steal anything from Wilcox."

"I certainly did not. I *gave* him stuff."

But a certain dreariness, a grey *malaise*, crept over him as Berners continued:

"I told you we had three scripts. You used an old one we discarded a year ago. Wilcox was in when your secretary arrived, and he sent one of them to you. Clever, eh?"

Pat was speechless.

"You see, he and that girl like each other. Seems she typed a play for him this summer."

"They like each other", said Pat incredulously. "Why, he —"

lay: cf. to lie, lay, lain
ever: *jamais*

get up on it: manage to do it
assignment: job
lost your grip: lost control
larceny: taking away other people's property □ **cunning:** skill, dexterity
nuts: crazy
steal: take away; to steal something *from* someone
laid out: prepared
whole: complete

like... better: prefer □ **ending:** end
pick up: understand
once: one time

stuff: ideas, material
dreariness: depression, sadness □ **crept:** infiltrated itself

discarded: abandoned □ **in:** in his office
clever: intelligent

was speechless: could find nothing to say
seems: it seems
play: for the theatre
incredulously: without believing it

"Hold it, Pat. You've had trouble enough today."

"He's responsible", Pat cried. "He wouldn't collaborate — and all the time —"

"— he was writing a swell script. And he can write his own ticket if we can persuade him to stay here and do another."

Pat could stand no more. He stood up.

"Anyhow thank you, Jack", he faltered. "Call my agent if anything turns up." Then he bolted suddenly and surprisingly for the door.

Jack Berners signaled on the Dictograph for the President's office.

"Get a chance to read it?" he asked in a tone of eagerness.

"It's swell. Better than you said. Wilcox is with me now."

"Have you signed him up?"

"I'm going to. Seems he wants to work with Hobby. Here, you talk to him."

Wilcox's rather high voice came over the wire.

"Must have Mike Hobby", he said. "Grateful to him. Had a quarrel with a certain young lady just before he came, but today Hobby brought us together. Besides I want to write a play about him. So give him to me — you fellows don't want him any more."

Berners picked up his secretary's phone.

"Go after Pat Hobby. He's probably in the bar across the street. We're putting him on salary again but we'll be sorry."

He switched off, switched on again.

"Oh! Take him his hat. He forgot his hat."

hold it: stop
cried: exclaimed
all the time: during that time
swell: wonderful
write his own ticket: do what stories he wants

Pat could stand no more: it was too much for Pat
anyhow: in any case □ **faltered:** said with hesitation
anything turns up: you have a job forme □ **bolted:** ran away

signaled on: called

eagerness: impatience, enthusiasm

signed him up: given him a contract
I'm going to: I'm going to give him a contract

over the wire: on the telephone
must have: I must have □ **grateful:** thankful
had: I had □ **quarrel:** conflict
brought us together: reconciled us □ **besides:** what is more

fellows: people

putting him on salary: giving him a job
we'll be sorry: we'll regret it
switched off, switched on: put down the receiver and picked it up

Grammaire au fil des nouvelles

En traduisant les phrases suivantes au moyen des structures suggérées en italiques entre parenthèses essayez de retrouver le texte anglais dont la page et la ligne sont indiquées par des chiffres : le premier renvoie à la page, le second à la ligne.

Pat Hobby n'était pas vexé, ni en tant qu'homme ni en tant qu'écrivain (*ni... ni...*, 48.4).

Tu avais beaucoup de succès auprès des secrétaires autrefois (**used to,** 50.1).

Je n'ai jamais écrit pour le cinéma (**present perfect,** 50.11).

Cela voulait dire qu'il pourrait avoir à travailler un peu (*modalité*, 50.13).

Il ne m'a pas encore donné de travail (**present perfect** ; *traduction de encore*, 52.32).

Il va probablement se mettre à vomir dans le bureau (*construction de* **start**, 54.3).

À la fin de la journée, il avait écrit deux pages de scénario (*génitif*, 56.10).

La peur stimula son cerveau (*construction de* **start**, 58.11).

Il fit quelques dizaines de petits changements (**dozen**, 60.24).

Mr. Berners aimerait avoir une copie pour trois heures et demie (**have**, 60.31).

Il avait pratiquement fait ce pour quoi il avait été engagé (**do** *de reprise*, 62.21).

Je ne lui ai rien volé (*construction de* **to steal**, 66.10).

PAT HOBBY AND ORSON WELLES

"Who's this Welles?" Pat asked of Louie, the studio bookie. "Every time I pick up a paper they got about this Welles."

"You know, he's that beard", explained Louie.

"Sure, I know he's that beard, you couldn't miss that. But what credits's he got? What's he done to draw one hundred and fifty grand a picture?"

What indeed? Had he, like Pat, been in Hollywood over twenty years? Did he have credits that would knock your eye out, extending up to — well, up to five years ago when Pat's credits had begun to be few and far between?

"Listen — they don't last long", said Louie consolingly, "We've seen 'em come and we've seen 'em go. Hey, Pat?"

Yes — but meanwhile those who had toiled in the vineyard through the heat of the day were lucky to get a few weeks at three-fifty. Men who had once had wives and Filipinos and swimming-pools.

"Maybe it's the beard", said Louie. "Maybe you and I should grow a beard. My father had a beard but it never got him off Grand Street."

The gift of hope had remained with Pat through his misfortunes — and the valuable alloy of his hope was proximity. Above all things one must stick around, one must be there when the glazed, tired mind of the producer grappled with the question "Who?" So presently Pat wandered out of the drugstore, and crossed the street to the lot that was home.

As he passed through the side entrance an unfamiliar studio policeman stood in his way.

"Everybody in the front entrance now."

"I'm Hobby, the writer", Pat said.

studio bookie: one man in the studio who takes money from people to bet on horses □ **pick up:** look at □ **got about:** mention

beard: (here) a man with hair on his face
miss: ignore
what credits's he got?: what films has he made? □ **draw:** get
grand: 1,000 dollars □ **a picture:** for one film
indeed: really □ **over:** more than
knock...out: impress you
extending up to...ago: until that period 5 years ago
few and far between: rare
last: to last, lasted, lasted; lasting: durable
seen 'em: seen them

meanwhile: during that time □ **toiled... the heat of the day:** worked hard in difficult circumstances; cf. a hot day
three-fifty: a weekly 350 dollars' salary □ **once:** at one time
Filipinos: servants from the Philippines □ **swimming-pools:** *piscines*

grow: to grow, grew, grown □ **grow a beard:** let a beard cover their faces □ **got him off Grand Street:** made him rich
gift: present; cf. to give □ **...with Pat:** Pat had never lost hope
misfortune: bad luck □ **valuable alloy:** principal element
above all things: more than anything else □ **stick around:** not go away □ **glazed:** fixed
grappled with: tried to solve □ **presently:** now
wandered out of: walked slowly out of □ **crossed:** went to the other side □ **lot:** studio area □ **that was home:** like his home
side entrance: ≠ front entrance
stood: to stand, stood, stood □ **in his way:** before him

writer: (here) script-writer

The Cossack was unimpressed.

"Got your card?"

"I'm between pictures. But I've got an engagement with Jack Berners."

"Front gate."

As he turned away Pat thought savagely: "Lousy Keystone Cop!" In his mind he shot it out with him. Plunk! the stomach. Plunk! Plunk! Plunk!

At the main entrance, too, there was a new face.

"Where's Ike?" Pat demanded.

"Ike's gone."

"Well, it's all right, I'm Pat Hobby. Ike always passes me."

"That's why he's gone", said the guardian blandly. "Who's your business with?"

Pat hesitated. He hated to disturb a producer.

"Call Jack Berners' office", he said. "Just speak to his secretary."

After a minute the man turned from the phone.

"What about?" he said.

"About a picture."

He waited for an answer.

"She wants to know what picture?"

"To hell with it", said Pat disgustedly. "Look — call Louie Griebel. What's all this about?"

"Orders from Mr. Kasper", said the clerk. "Last week a visitor from Chicago fell in the wind machine — Hello. Mr. Louie Griebel?"

"I'll talk to him", said Pat, taking the phone.

"I can't do nothing, Pat", mourned Louie. "I had trouble getting my boy in this morning. Some twirp from Chicago fell in the wind machine."

Cossack: *Cosaque* (ironical) ☐ **unimpressed:** indifferent
got your card: have you got your card
...pictures: I'm not working at the moment ☐ **engagement:** appointment
front gate: front entrance
turned away: went away ☐ **lousy Keystone Cops:** incompetent police force in film comedies ☐ **shot it out:** had a gun fight
plunk: sound made by impact of bullet
main: chief, principal

...passes me: lets me get in

blandly: (here) ironically
hated: did not like ☐ **to disturb:** to trouble ☐ **producer:** the man who produces and finances films

what about: what (do you want to see him) about
picture: motion picture, movie, film

to hell with it: never mind ☐ **disgustedly:** (here) with indignation
...about?: what's going on?
clerk: employee
wind machine: that imitates sound of wind for the sound effects in films

...nothing: anything ☐ **mourned:** said with regret
getting...in: getting the boy into the lot ☐ **twirp:** idiot
fell: to fall, fell, fallen

"What's that got to do with me?" demanded Pat vehemently.

He walked, a little faster than his wont, along the studio wall to the point where it joined the back lot. There was a guard there but there were always people passing to and fro and he joined one of the groups. Once inside he would see Jack and have himself excepted from this absurd ban. Why, he had known this lot when the first shacks were rising on it, when this was considered the edge of the desert.

"Sorry mister, you with this party?"

"I'm in a hurry", said Pat. "I've lost my card."

"Yeah? Well, for all I know you may be a plain clothes man." He held open a copy of a photo magazine under Pat's nose, "I wouldn't let you in even if you told me you was this here Orson Welles."

II

There is an old Chaplin picture about a crowded street-car where the entrance of one man at the rear forces another out in front. A similar image came into Pat's mind in the ensuing days whenever he thought of Orson Welles. Welles was in; Hobby was out. Never before had the studio been barred to Pat and though Welles was on another lot it seemed as if his large body, pushing in brashly from nowhere, had edged Pat out the gate.

"Now where do you go?" Pat thought. He had worked in the other studios but they were not his. At this studio

what's it got to do with me?: how does it concern me?

than his wont: than usual
the back lot: the studio at the back
to and fro: coming and going
once inside: when he was inside the studio
excepted from: exempted from
ban: interdiction □ **shacks:** huts, primitive buildings
were rising: were being built □ **the edge:** the frontier

you with this party: are you with this party
I've lost: to lose, lost, lost; to be lost; a great loss
for all I know: as far as I'm concerned □ **plain clothes man:** a policeman in ordinary clothes □ **he held:** to hold, held, held
let you in: permit you to come in □ **even if:** *même si*
was: (infml.) were □ **this here:** this man

picture: film, movie □ **crowded:** full of people □ **streetcar:** tramway □ **at the rear:** at the back □ **another:** another man

ensuing days: the days after □ **whenever:** when □ **thought:** to think, thought, thought □ **in:** successful □ **out:** finished
barred: forbidden, prohibited, closed □ **though:** even if
as if: that □ **brashly:** vulgarly
...nowhere: arriving as a complete stranger □ **edged:** pushed □ **out the gate:** out of the gate □ **where do you go:** what shall I do
his: his studio

he never felt unemployed — in recent times of stress he had eaten property food on its stages — half a cold lobster during a scene from *The Divine Miss Carstairs*; he had often slept on the sets and last winter made use of a Chesterfield overcoat from the costume department. Orson Welles had no business edging him out of this. Orson Welles belonged with the rest of the snobs back in New York.

On the third day he was frantic with gloom. He had sent note after note to Jack Berners and even asked Louie to intercede — now word came that Jack had left town. There were so few friends left. Desolate, he stood in front of the automobile gate with a crowd of staring children, feeling that he had reached the end at last.

A great limousine rolled out, in the back of which Pat recognized the great overstuffed Roman face of Harold Marcus. The car rolled toward the children and, as one of them ran in front of it, slowed down. The old man spoke into the tube and the car halted. He leaned out blinking.

"Is there no policeman here?" he asked of Pat.

"No, Mr. Marcus", said Pat quickly. "There should be. I'm Pat Hobby, the writer — could you give me a lift down the street?"

It was unprecedented — it was an act of desperation but Pat's need was great.

Mr. Marcus looked at him closely.

"Oh yes, I remember you", he said. "Get in."

He might possibly have meant get up in front with the chauffeur. Pat compromised by opening one of the little seats. Mr. Marcus was one of the most powerful men in the whole picture world. He did not occupy himself with production any longer. He spent most of his time rocking

stress: tension
eaten: to eat, ate, eaten □ **property food:** food used in film scenes
stages: *plateaux* □ **lobster:** *homard*
sets: built-up scenes □ **Chesterfield overcoat:** warm coat for winter wear
no business: no right □ **edging:** pushing □ **belonged:** was in his proper place □ **back:** over there
frantic: crazy □ **gloom:** melancholy
note after note: one letter after another
word came: there came news □ **left town:** to leave, left, left
so few friends left: Pat did not have many friends □ **stood:** to stand, stood, stood □ **staring:** looking fixedly
he had reached: he had arrived at □ **at last:** finally
rolled out: moved forward □ **in the back of which:** in the back of the car □ **overstuffed:** too fat, corpulent

slowed down: reduced speed □ **spoke:** to speak, spoke, spoken
tube: gadget used to talk to the driver □ **leaned:** inclined his body
blinking: with eyes opening and shutting

give me a lift: take me in your car
down the street: to go down the street
unprecedented: without any precedent □ **desperation:** despair

closely: with great attention

meant: to mean, meant, meant □ **get up with the chauffeur:** sit with the chauffeur □ **compromised:** made a concession
powerful: strong, influential
whole: entire
spent: to spend, spent, spent □ **rocking:** travelling

from coast to coast on fast trains, merging and launching, launching and merging, like a much divorced woman.

"Some day those children'll get hurt."

"Yes, Mr. Marcus", agreed Pat heartily. "Mr. Marcus —"

"They ought to have a policeman there."

"Yes, Mr. Marcus. Mr. Marcus —"

"Hm-m-m!" said Mr. Marcus. "Where do you want to be dropped?"

Pat geared himself to work fast.

"Mr. Marcus, when I was your press agent —"

"I know", said Mr. Marcus. "You wanted a ten dollar a week raise."

"What a memory!" cried Pat in gladness. "What a memory! But Mr. Marcus, now I don't want anything at all."

"This is a miracle."

"I've got modest wants, see, and I've saved enough to retire."

He thrust his shoes slightly forward under a hanging blanket. The Chesterfield coat effectively concealed the rest.

"That's what I'd like", said Mr. Marcus gloomily. "A farm — with chickens. Maybe a little nine-hole course. Not even a stock-ticker."

"I want to retire, but different", said Pat earnestly. "Pictures have been my life. I want to watch them grow and grow —"

Mr. Marcus groaned.

"Till they explode", he said. "Look at Fox! I cried for him." He pointed to his eyes, "Tears!"

Pat nodded very sympathetically.

fast: express □ **merging and launching:** buying and creating firms
much: (here) often
'll get hurt: will be hit by a car
heartily: warmly, with conviction

they ought to have: there should be

to be dropped: to be left
geared himself: prepared himself □ **fast:** quickly
your press agent: the person who represented you when meeting with the press
a week: every week □ **raise:** increase, augmentation
in gladness: happily
I don't want anything at all: I want absolutely nothing

wants: needs □ **I've saved enough:** I've accumulated enough money
to retire: to stop working
thrust: pushed □ **slightly forward:** a little in front of him
hanging blanket: large woollen sheet covering the seat □ **concealed the rest:** made the rest of his clothes invisible
I'd like: I would like □ **gloomily:** with melancholy
chickens: *poulets* □ **nine-hole course:** golf-links; where golf is played
stock-ticker: machine that gives value of stocks (*actions en Bourse*)
earnestly: seriously
pictures: films, movies
grow: expand; to grow, grew, grown
groaned: made a sound expressing disapproval
till: until □ **Fox:** William Fox created the 20th Century Fox studio in 1915 □ **I cried for him:** I pitied him, I wept for him □ **pointed to:** showed □ **tears:** *larmes* □ **nodded:** agreed

"I want only one thing." From the long familiarity he went into the foreign locution. "I should go on the lot anytime. From nothing. Only to be there. Should bother nobody. Only help a little from nothing if any young person wants advice."

"See Berners", said Marcus.

"He said see you."

"Then you did want something", Marcus smiled. "All right, all right by me. Where do you get off now?"

"Could you write me a pass?" Pat pleaded. "Just a word on your card?"

"I'll look into it", said Mr. Marcus. "Just now I've got things on my mind. I'm going to a luncheon." He sighed profoundly. "They want I should meet this new Orson Welles that's in Hollywood."

Pat's heart winced. There it was again — that name, sinister and remorseless, spreading like a dark cloud over all his skies.

"Mr. Marcus", he said so sincerely that his voice trembled, "I wouldn't be surprised if Orson Welles is the biggest menace that's come to Hollywood for years. He gets a hundred and fifty grand a picture and I wouldn't be surprised if he was so radical that you had to have all new equipment and start all over again like you did with sound in 1928."

"Oh my God!" groaned Mr. Marcus.

"And me", said Pat, "all I want is a pass and no money — to leave things as they are."

Mr. Marcus reached for his card case.

he went...locution: he spoke English like a foreigner
lot: studio
anytime: at any time ☐ **from nothing:** for nothing
should bother nobody: I wouldn't create any trouble
young person: (here) inexperienced script-writer ☐ **advice:** guidance, help
he said see you: he said that I should see you
you did want: you really wanted
all right by me: I have no objection ☐ **get off:** stop
a pass: an entrance permit ☐ **pleaded:** implored

look into it: think about it later
things on my mind: problems ☐ **luncheon:** lunch ☐ **sighed:** made a sound expressing sadness ☐ **They want I should meet:** they want me to meet
winced: experienced pain
remorseless: pitiless, cruel ☐ **spreading:** extending
over all his skies: over his horizon

that's come: that has come
gets: receives ☐ **a hundred and fifty grand:** 150,000 dollars
radical: revolutionary ☐ **you had to have:** you would be obliged to get ☐ **sound:** sound films had succeeded silent ones in 1927

groaned: made an inarticulate sound expressing despair
all I want: the only thing I want
to leave things as they are: to make no changes
reached for: made a move to take out

III

To those grouped together under the name 'talent', the atmosphere of a studio is not unfailingly bright — one fluctuates too quickly between high hope and grave apprehension. Those few who decide things are happy in their work and sure that they are worthy of their hire — the rest live in a mist of doubt as to when their vast inadequacy will be disclosed.

Pat's psychology was, oddly, that of the masters and for the most part he was unworried even though he was off salary. But there was one large fly in the ointment — for the first time in his life he began to feel a loss of identity. Due to reasons that he did not quite understand, though it might have been traced to his conversation, a number of people began to address him as 'Orson.'

Now to lose one's identity is a careless thing in any case. But to lose it to an enemy, or at least to one who has become scapegoat for our misfortunes — that is a hardship. Pat was *not* Orson. Any resemblance must be faint and farfetched and he was aware of the fact. The final effect was to make him, in that regard, something of an eccentric.

"Pat", said Joe the barber, "Orson was in here today and asked me to trim his beard."

"I hope you set fire to it", said Pat.

"I did", Joe winked at waiting customers over a hot towel. "He asked for a singe so I took it all off. Now his face is as bald as yours. In fact you look a bit alike."

This was the morning the kidding was so ubiquitous that, to avoid it, Pat lingered in Mario's bar across the

to those: for the people □ **'talent':** promising and talented actors and writers □ **not unfailingly bright:** not always pleasant

those few: the few people
they are worthy of their hire: they merit their salaries
mist: cloud, vapour □ **doubt:** uncertainty □ **as to:** concerning
disclosed: made public
oddly: strangely □ **that of:** the psychology of □ **for the most part:** essentially □ **unworried:** unperturbed □ **even though:** even if □ **off salary:** without a salary □ **fly in the ointment:** frustration
a loss: privation; cf. to lose, lost, lost
due to: because of □ **quite:** completely
traced to: attributed to, because of
a number of people: many people □ **address him:** call him
careless: negligent □ **in any case:** in any situation
to lose it to an enemy: to abandon it to an enemy
scapegoat: person held unjustly responsible □ **misfortunes:** unhappiness, bad luck □ **hardship:** severe suffering
faint: indistinct □ **farfetched:** (here) unbelievable □ **aware:** conscious □ **in that regard:** in that respect □ **something of an eccentric:** a little eccentric

trim: cut; to cut, cut, cut
set fire to: burn; to set, set, set
winked: closed one eye quickly □ **hot towel:** hot serviette
for a singe: to trim his beard by burning it □ **took...off:** cut it all off □ **bald:** without a hair □ **look alike:** resemble each other
kidding: jokes □ **ubiquitous:** omnipresent
avoid it: escape from it □ **lingered:** spent a long time

street. He was not drinking — at the bar, that is, for he was down to his last thirty cents, but he refreshed himself frequently from a half-pint in his back pocket. He needed the stimulus for he had to make a touch presently and he knew that money was easier to borrow when one didn't have an air of urgent need.

His quarry, Jeff Boldini, was in an unsympathetic state of mind. He too was an artist, albeit a successful one, and a certain great lady of the screen had just burned him up by criticizing a wig he had made for her. He told the story to Pat at length and the latter waited until it was all out before broaching his request.

"No soap", said Jeff. "Hell, you never paid me back what you borrowed last month."

"But I got a job now", lied Pat. "This is just to tide me over. I start tomorrow."

"If they don't give the job to Orson Welles", said Jeff humorously.

Pat's eyes narrowed but he managed to utter a polite, borrower's laugh.

"Hold it", said Jeff. "You know I think you look like him?"

"Yeah."

"Honest. Anyhow I could make you look like him. I could make you a beard that would be his double."

"I wouldn't be his double for fifty grand."

With his head on one side Jeff regarded Pat.

"I could", he said. "Come on in to my chair and let me see."

"Like hell."

"Come on. I'd like to try it. You haven't got anything to do. You don't work till tomorrow."

that is: that is to say
he was down to: he had only
a half-pint: a flask of whisky
to make a touch: to try to borrow money
money was easier to borrow: it was easier to borrow money

quarry: prey, target ☐ **unsympathetic:** hostile ☐ **state of mind:** mood, temper ☐ **albeit:** though
the screen: (here) the cinema ☐ **burned him up:** infuriated
wig: false hair
at length: in detail ☐ **the latter:** Pat ☐ **all out:** finished
broaching: introducing
no soap: (fam.) certainly not ☐ **hell:** interjection ☐ **paid me back:** reimbursed me
I got: I've got ☐ **lied:** said untruthfully ☐ **tide me over:** help me during a difficult period

humorously: joking
narrowed: nearly closed ☐ **managed to utter:** could just emit

hold it: wait a second

honest: honestly, frankly ☐ **anyhow:** in any case ☐ **look like:** resemble
I wouldn't be: I wouldn't want to be ☐ **grand:** 1,000 dollars
his head on one side: inclined on one side

like hell: never
you haven't got anything to do: you have got nothing to do
till: until

"I don't want a beard."

"It'll come off."

"I don't want it."

"It won't cost you anything. In fact I'll be paying you — I'll loan you the ten smackers if you'll let me make you a beard."

Half an hour later Jeff looked at his completed work.

"It's perfect", he said. "Not only the beard but the eyes and everything."

"All right. Now take it off", said Pat moodily.

"What's the hurry? That's a fine muff. That's a work of art. We ought to put a camera on it. Too bad you're working tomorrow — they're using a dozen beards out on Sam Jones' set and one of them went to jail in a homo raid. I bet with that muff you could get the job."

It was weeks since Pat had heard the word job and he could not himself say how he managed to exist and eat. Jeff saw the light in his eye.

"What say? Let me drive you out there just for fun", pleaded Jeff. "I'd like to see if Sam could tell it was a phony muff."

"I'm a writer, not a ham."

"Come on! Nobody would never know you back of that. And you'd draw another ten bucks."

As they left the make-up department Jeff lingered behind a minute. On a strip of cardboard he crayoned the name Orson Welles in large block letters. And outside without Pat's notice, he stuck it in the windshield of his car.

He did not go directly to the back lot. Instead he drove not too swiftly up the main studio street. In front of the administration building he stopped on the pretext that the engine was missing, and almost in no time a small but

it'll come off: you'll be able to take it off

cost: to cost, cost, cost
loan: lend, give □ **smackers:** (sl) dollars

completed: finished

moodily: unsmiling, morose
what's the hurry?: why so soon? □ **fine muff:** beautiful beard
to put a camera on it: to film it □ **too bad:** it's a pity
using: employing □ **beards:** bearded men
set: *plateau, décor* □ **jail:** prison □ **homo:** homosexual
I bet: I'm sure

the light in his eyes: the light of hope in his eyes
what say: what do you say? □ **for fun:** as a joke
pleaded: implored □ **if Sam could tell:** if Sam could see
phony: false
ham: (slang) actor
back of that: behind that beard
draw: get □ **another:** an additional □ **bucks:** (sl) dollars
left: went out of □ **make-up:** cosmetics □ **lingered:** waited
strip: rectangular piece □ **cardboard:** *carton*
block: capital □ **without Pat's notice:** without Pat noticing it
stuck: fixed with glue □ **windshield:** *pare-brise*
back lot: studio at the back □ **instead:** in place of □ **drove:** to drive, drove, driven □ **not too swiftly:** not too fast
the engine was missing: *le moteur avait des ratés*
almost: practically □ **in no time:** immediately

definitely interested crowd began to gather. But Jeff's plans did not include stopping anywhere long, so he hopped in and they started on a tour around the commissary.

"Where are we going?" demanded Pat.

He had already made one nervous attempt to tear the beard from him, but to his surprise it did not come away.

He complained of this to Jeff.

"Sure", Jeff explained. "That's made to last. You'll have to soak it off."

The car paused momentarily at the door of the commissary. Pat saw blank eyes staring at him and he stared back at them blankly from the rear seat.

"You'd think I was the only beard on the lot", he said gloomily.

"You can sympathize with Orson Welles."

"To hell with him."

This colloquy would have puzzled those without, to whom he was nothing less than the real McCoy.

Jeff drove on slowly up the street. Ahead of them a little group of men were walking — one of them, turning, saw the car and drew the attention of the others to it. Whereupon the most elderly member of the party threw up his arms in what appeared to be a defensive gesture, and plunged to the sidewalk as the car went past.

"My God, did you see that?" exclaimed Jeff. "That was Mr. Marcus."

He came to a stop. An excited man ran up and put his head in the car window.

"Mr. Welles, our Mr. Marcus has had a heart attack. Can we use your car to get him to the infirmary?"

Pat stared. Then very quickly he opened the door on

crowd: group of people ☐ **gather:** assemble
hopped in: jumped into the car
commissary: cafeteria

made one...attempt: tried ☐ **tear:** detach, unstick, pull off
come away: come off
complained: expressed dissatisfaction
made to last: very resistant
soak it off: leave it in water for some time

blank: uncomprehending ☐ **staring:** looking fixedly
blankly: without expression ☐ **rear:** back
you'd think: one would think ☐ **beard:** man with a beard
gloomily: with melancholy

to hell with him: *qu'il aille au diable*
colloquy: conversation ☐ **puzzled:** disconcerted
the real McCoy: the real thing, the real Orson Welles
ahead: in front of

drew: attracted ☐ **whereupon:** at his
the most elderly: the oldest ☐ **threw up his arms:** raised his arms above his head ☐ **gesture:** movement
plunged to: fell down on ☐ **sidewalk:** (Am.); pavement (GB)

came to a stop: stopped ☐ **ran up:** ran towards them

stared: looked fixedly at the man

the other side and dashed from the car. Not even the beard could impede his streamlined flight. The policeman at the gate, not recognizing the incarnation, tried to have words with him but Pat shook him off with the ease of a triple-threat back and never paused till he reached Mario's bar.

Three extras with beards stood at the rail, and with relief Pat merged himself into their corporate whiskers. With a trembling hand he took the hard-earned ten dollar bill from his pocket.

"Set 'em up", he cried hoarsely. "Every muff has a drink on me."

dashed: ran away
impede: stop □ **streamlined flight:** rapid, energetic escape
the incarnation: the resemblance □ **to have words:** to argue with
shook him off: was quicker than him □ **ease:** facility
triple-threat back: football player that is good at running, kicking and forward passing
extras: *figurants* □ **rail:** bar □ **relief:** deliverance from anxiety
merged: dissimulated □ **corporate:** belonging to the same group □ **whiskers:** moustaches, beards □ **earned:** gained □ **bill:** bank note

set 'em up: bring out the glasses □ **muff:** bearded man
a drink on me: a drink paid by me

Grammaire au fil des nouvelles

En traduisant les phrases suivantes au moyen des structures suggérées en italiques entre parenthèses essayez de retrouver le texte anglais dont la page et la ligne sont indiquées par des chiffres : le premier renvoie à la page, le second à la ligne.

Peut-être devrions-nous nous laisser pousser la barbe (*traduction de devoir ; traduction de se laisser + verbe...* 72.20).

J'ai eu du mal à faire entrer mon employé ce matin (*avoir du mal + gérondif,* 74.30).

Jamais auparavant le studio n'avait été fermé à Pat (*inversion après négations,* 76.28).

Il lui restait tellement peu d'amis (*quantifieurs,* 78.11).

La moitié d'un homard froid... (*traduction de moitié,* 78.2).

Il n'y a pas d'agent ici ? — Non, mais il devrait y en avoir un (*traduction de devoir ; ellipse,* 78.20,21).

Mr. Marcus était l'homme le plus puissant de tout le monde du cinéma (*superlatif,* 78.30).

Ils devraient mettre un agent à cet endroit (*traduction de devoir,* 80.6).

Il passait son temps à faire la navette d'une côte à l'autre (*gérondif,* 78.32).

Quelle mémoire ! (*exclamatifs,* 80.14).

Tu ne m'as jamais remboursé ce que tu m'as emprunté le mois dernier (*temps du passé,* 86.13).

THE HOMES OF THE STARS

Beneath a great striped umbrella at the side of a boulevard in a Hollywood heat wave, sat a man. His name was Gus Venske (no relation to the runner) and he wore magenta pants, cerise shoes and a sport article from Vine Street which resembled nothing so much as a cerulean blue pajama top.

Gus Venske was not a freak nor were his clothes at all extraordinary for his time and place. He had a profession — on a pole beside the umbrella was a placard:

VISIT THE HOMES OF THE STARS

Business was bad or Gus would not have hailed the unprosperous man who stood in the street beside a panting, steaming car, anxiously watching its efforts to cool.

'Hey fella,' said Gus, without much hope. 'Wanna visit the homes of the stars?'

The red-rimmed eyes of the watcher turned from the automobile and looked superciliously upon Gus.

'I'm *in* pictures,' said the man, 'I'm in 'em myself.'

'Actor?'

'No. Writer.'

Pat Hobby turned back to his car, which was whistling like a peanut wagon. He had told the truth — or what was once the truth. Often in the old days his name had flashed on the screen for the few seconds allotted to authorship, but for the past five years his services had been less and less in demand.

Presently Gus Venske shut up shop for lunch by putting his folders and maps into a briefcase and walking off with it under his arm. As the sun grew hotter moment by moment, Pat Hobby took refuge under the faint protection

beneath: under □ **great:** big □ **striped:** *rayé* □ **at the side of:** near
heat wave: a series of hot days
no relation: member of the same family □ **magenta:** brilliant red
pants: trousers □ **cerise:** red
nothing so much: very much □ **cerulean:** deep blue
pajama top: *haut de pyjama*
a freak: abnormal □ **nor were his clothes:** his clothes were not... either □ **his time and place:** his situation
pole: *poteau* □ **placard:** poster

...was bad: there were not many customers □ **hailed:** called
unprosperous: not rich □ **panting:** making abnormal noises
steaming: emitting vapour □ **its:** the car's □ **cool:** get colder
fella: fellow □ **wanna:** do you want to

red-rimmed eyes: red eyes □ **watcher:** the man watching
looked... upon: looked at □ **superciliously:** in a superior manner
in: working in □ **'em:** them

writer: scriptwriter
whistling: making a hissing sound
peanut wagon: cart used to dispense peanuts in the streets
once: in the past □ **the truth:** a real fact □ **flashed:** appeared
few: not many □ **allotted:** allocated □ **authorship:** authors of the script
in demand: required
presently: soon □ **shut up shop:** stopped working
folders: brochures □ **briefcase:** small bag □ **walking off:** walking away □ **grew:** got; to grow, grew, grown
took: to take, took, taken □ **faint:** small

of the umbrella and inspected a soiled folder which had been dropped by Mr. Venske. If Pat had not been down to his last fourteen cents he would have telephoned a garage for aid — as it was, he could only wait.

After a while a limousine with a Missouri license drew to rest beside him. Behind the chauffeur sat a little white moustached man and a large woman with a small dog. They conversed for a moment — then, in a rather shame-faced way, the woman leaned out and addressed Pat.

'What stars' homes can you visit?' she asked.

It took a moment for this to sink in.

'I mean can we go to Robert Taylor's home and Clark Gable's and Shirley Temple's —'

'I guess you can if you can get in,' said Pat.

'Because —' continued the woman, '— if we could go to the very best homes, the most exclusive — we would be prepared to pay more than your regular price.'

Light dawned upon Pat. Here together were suckers and smackers. Here was that dearest of Hollywood dreams — the angle. If one got the right angle it meant meals at the Brown Derby, long nights with bottles and girls, a new tire for his old car. And here was an angle fairly thrusting itself at him.

He rose and went to the side of the limousine.

'Sure. Maybe I could fix it.' As he spoke he felt a pang of doubt. 'Would you be able to pay in advance?'

The couple exchanged a look.

'Suppose we gave you five dollars now,' the woman said, 'and five dollars if we can visit Clark Gable's home or somebody like that.'

Once upon a time such a thing would have been so

inspected: looked closely at □ **soiled:** dirty
dropped: let fall □ **down to:** reduced to
cents: one cent is one hundreth of a dollar
as it was: in his situation
while: moment □ **license:** *plaque minéralogique* □ **drew to rest:** stopped □ **beside:** near □ **behind:** at the back of
white moustached: with a white moustache
conversed: talked □ **rather:** a little
shame-faced: looking ashamed, humble, shy □ **leaned out:** inclined her head out of the car window

for this to sink in: for him to understand the situation
Robert Taylor... Clark Gable: American film actors
Shirley Temple: American child star of the thirties
guess: suppose □ **get in:** get into their homes

exclusive: select
regular: usual
light dawned upon him: Pat suddenly understood □ **suckers:** fools
smackers: slang for dollars □ **dearest:** favourite
angle: opportunity, chance □ **meant:** signified
meals: lunches, dinners □ **Brown Derby:** famous Los Angeles restaurant □ **tire:** pneumatic tire (also **tyre)**
fairly: practically □ **thrusting... at him:** imposing itself
rose: stood up; to rise
fix: arrange □ **felt:** to feel □ **pang:** sudden and unpleasant feeling
doubt: uncertainty
exchanged a look: looked at each other

once upon a time: in the past

easy. In his salad days when Pat had twelve or fifteen writing credits a year, he could have called up many people who would have said, 'Sure, Pat, if it means anything to you.' But now he could only think of a handful who really recognized him and spoke to him around the lots — Melvyn Douglas and Robert Young and Ronald Colman and Young Doug. Those he had known best had retired or passed away.

And he did not know except vaguely where the new stars lived, but he had noticed that on the folder were typewritten several dozen names and addresses with penciled checks after each.

'Of course you can't be sure anybody's at home,' he said, 'they might be working in the studios.'

'We understand that.' The lady glanced at Pat's car, glanced away. 'We'd better go in our motor.'

'Sure.'

Pat got up in front with the chauffeur — trying to think fast. The actor who spoke to him most pleasantly was Ronald Colman — they had never exchanged more than conventional salutations but he might pretend that he was calling to interest Colman in a story.

Better still, Colman was probably not at home and Pat might wangle his clients an inside glimpse of the house. Then the process might be repeated at Robert Young's house and Young Doug's and Melvyn Douglas'. By that time the lady would have forgotten Gable and the afternoon would be over.

He looked at Ronald Colman's address on the folder and gave the direction to the chauffeur.

'We know a woman who had her picture taken with

in his salad days: when he was young
...writing credits: when Pat made 12 or 15 films in a year
if it means anything to you: if it is important to you
a handful: very few actors; cf. hand
lots: studios ☐ **Melvyn Douglas... Robert Young... Ronald Colman:** American actors ☐ **Young Doug:** Douglas Fairbanks Junior, American actor ☐ **retired:** stopped working ☐ **passed away:** died

noticed: seen ☐ **typewritten:** printed
penciled checks: marks written in pencil
each: *chacun*
anybody: any of the actors on the list

glanced: looked briefly
glanced away: *détourna les yeux* ☐ **we'd better go:** it would be better for us to go
got up: got into the car and sat down ☐ **trying:** cf. to try
most pleasantly: in the most pleasant manner
they: Ronald Colman and Pat Hobby
he might pretend: it was possible to pretend; cf. may
calling: paying a visit ☐ **interest... in:** get him interested in

better still: even better
wangle: manage to obtain for ☐ **inside glimpse:** quick view of the inside of the house ☐ **process:** action
Young Doug's: Douglas Fairbanks Junior's house ☐ **Melvyn Douglas':** Melvyn Douglas' house ☐ **by that time:** when they had done all that ☐ **forgotten:** cf. to forget ☐ **be over:** have ended

picture: photograph

George Brent,' said the lady as they started off, 'Mrs. Horace J. Ives, Jr.'

'She's our neighbor,' said her husband. 'She lives at 372 Rose Drive in Kansas City. And we live at 327.'

'She had her picture taken with George Brent. We always wondered if she had to pay for it. Of course I don't know that I'd want to go so far as *that*. I don't know what they'd say back home.'

'I don't think we want to go as far as all that,' agreed her husband.

'Where are we going first?' asked the lady, cosily.

'Well, I had a couple calls to pay anyhow,' said Pat. 'I got to see Ronald Colman about something.'

'Oh, he's one of my favorites. Do you know him well?'

'Oh yes,' said Pat, 'I'm not in this business regularly. I'm just doing it today for a friend. I'm a writer.'

Sure in the knowledge that not so much as a trio of picture writers were known to the public he named himself as the author of several recent successes.

'That's very interesting,' said the man, 'I knew a writer once — this Upton Sinclair or Sinclair Lewis. Not a bad fellow even if he was a socialist.'

'Why aren't you writing a picture now?' asked the lady.

'Well, you see we're on strike,' Pat invented. 'We got a thing called the Screen Playwriters' Guild and we're on strike.'

'Oh.' His clients stared with suspicion at this emissary of Stalin in the front seat of their car.

'What are you striking for?' asked the man uneasily.

Pat's political development was rudimentary. He hesitated.

George Brent: Hollywood actor ☐ **off:** to drive
Jr: Junior
neighbor: person living next door; (GB) neighbour
drive: road
picture: photograph ☐ **taken:** to take, took, taken
wondered: wanted to know ☐ **I don't know that I'd want:** I don't think I really want ☐ **so far as:** as far as
they'd say: they would say ☐ **back home:** in Kansas City
agreed: cf. to agree

cosily: happily
a couple calls to pay: two or three visits to make ☐ **anyhow:** in any case ☐ **I got:** I've got
favorites: favorite actors

this business: showing the homes of the stars
writer: script writer
sure in the knowledge: being quite sure ☐ **not so much:** not even
picture: film ☐ **known:** cf. to know ☐ **named himself as:** said he was
successes: sing. success

once: at a time ☐ **Upton Sinclair... Sinclair Lewis:** American novelists who wrote on social themes ☐ **fellow:** man

we're on strike: we've stopped work voluntarily ☐ **got:** we've got
Screen Playwriters: writers who write scenarios

stared: looked fixedly ☐ **emissary:** person sent on a mission
Stalin: Joseph Stalin (1879-1953) ruler of the Soviet Union from 1929 to his death ☐ **striking:** on strike ☐ **uneasily:** feeling uncomfortable ☐ **...was rudimentary:** Pat did not know much about politics

'Oh, better living conditions,' he said finally, 'free pencils and paper. I don't know — it's all in the Wagner Act.' After a moment he added vaguely, 'Recognize Finland.'

'I didn't know writers had unions,' said the man. 'Well, if you're on strike who writes the movies?'

'The producers', said Pat bitterly. 'That's why they're so lousy'.

'Well, that's what I would call an odd state of things.'

They came in sight of Ronald Colman's house and Pat swallowed uneasily. A shining new roadster sat out in front.

'I better go in first,' he said. 'I mean we wouldn't want to come in on any — on any family scene or anything.'

'Does he have family scenes?' asked the lady eagerly.

'Oh, well, you know how people are,' said Pat with charity. 'I think I ought to see how things are first.'

The car stopped. Drawing a long breath Pat got out. At the same moment the door of the house opened and Ronald Colman hurried down the walk. Pat's heart missed a beat as the actor glanced in his direction.

'Hello Pat', he said. Evidently he had no notion that Pat was a caller for he jumped into his car and the sound of his motor drowned out Pat's responses as he drove away.

'Well, he called you "Pat"', said the woman impressed.

'I guess he was in a hurry', said Pat. 'But maybe we could see his house.'

He rehearsed a speech going up the walk. He had just spoken to his friend Mr. Colman, and received permission to look around.

But the house was shut and locked and there was no answer to the bell. He would have to try Melvyn Douglas

free: that you don't have to pay for
Wagner Act: the National Labor Relations Act (1935) gave workers the right to organize □ **recognize:** acknowledge the *de facto* existence of; Finland became a republic in 1919
unions: trade unions; organized associations of workers to protect and promote their interests □ **movies:** films
producers: who finance films □ **bitterly:** with resentment
lousy: bad
odd: strange, surprising □ **state of things:** situation
in sight of: near enough to see
swallowed: *avala sa salive* □ **uneasily:** apprehensively □ **shining:** splendid □ **roadster:** *décapotable* □ **sat out:** was waiting
I better: I'd better
to come in on: to interrupt □ **scene:** quarrel □ **anything:** things like that □ **eagerly:** full of curiosity

I ought to: it would be better to □ **how things are:** what the situation is like □ **drawing a long breath:** breathing deeply

hurried down: walked quickly along □ **walk:** pavement
missed a beat: nearly stopped □ **as:** when □ **glanced:** looked briefly
no notion: no idea
caller: visitor □ **car:** motor car
drowned out: made... inaudible □ **responses:** answers □ **drove away:** went away in his car; cf. to drive
guess: think

rehearsed: repeated to himself □ **going up:** walking along

look around: make a tour of the house
shut: closed
bell: *sonnerie*

whose salutations, on second thought, were a little warmer than Ronald Colman's. At any rate his clients' faith in him was now firmly founded. The 'Hello, Pat', rang confidently in their ears; by proxy they were already inside the charmed circle.

'Now let's try Clark Gable's', said the lady. 'I'd like to tell Carole Lombard about her hair.'

The lese majesty made Pat's stomach wince. Once in a crowd he had met Clark Gable but he had no reason to believe that Mr. Gable remembered.

'Well, we could try Melvyn Douglas' first and then Bob Young or else Young Doug. They're all on the way. You see Gable and Lombard live away out in the St Joaquin valley.'

'Oh,' said the lady disappointed, 'I did want to run up and see their bedroom. Well then, our next choice would be Shirley Temple.' She looked at her little dog. 'I know that would be Boojie's choice too.'

'They're kind of afraid of kidnappers,' said Pat.

Ruffled, the man produced his business card and handed is to Pat.

DEERING R. ROBINSON
Vice President and Chairman
of the Board
Robdeer Food Products

'Does *that* sound as if I want to kidnap Shirley Temple?'

'They just have to be sure', said Pat apologetically. 'After we go to Melvyn —'

'No — let's see Shirley Temple's *now*', insisted the

on second thought: after reflection ☐ **warmer:** more cordial
at any rate: anyway ☐ **faith:** belief
was... firmly founded: had a firm basis ☐ **rang:** resounded, echoed
confidently: in a reassuring manner ☐ **by proxy:** *par procuration* ☐
inside: members of ☐ **charmed circle:** elite
Clark Gable's: Clark Gable's house
tell... about: advise ☐ **Carole Lombard:** actress, married to Gable
lese majesty: disrespect ☐ **wince:** suffer ☐ **once:** on one occasion
crowd: great number of people ☐ **met:** cf. to meet

Melvyn Douglas': Melvyn Douglas' house

away: a long way away

I did want: I really wanted ☐ **run up:** go upstairs
next: second ☐ **choice:** cf. to choose

Boojie: the little dog
kind of: rather
ruffled: angry ☐ **handed:** gave

Chairman of the Board: *Président du Conseil d'Administration*

sound as if: look as if

apologetically: trying to make excuses

let's see: let us see

woman. 'Really! I told you in the first place what I wanted.'

Pat hesitated.

'First I'll have to stop in some drugstore and phone about it.'

In a drugstore he exchanged some of the five dollars for a half pint of gin and took two long swallows behind a high counter, after which he considered the situation. He could, of course, duck Mr. and Mrs. Robinson immediately — after all he had produced Ronald Colman, with sound, for their five smackers. On the other hand they just *might* catch Miss Temple on her way in or out — and for a pleasant day at Santa Anita tomorrow Pat needed five smackers more. In the glow of the gin his courage mounted, and returning to the limousine he gave the chauffeur the address.

But approaching the Temple house his spirit quailed as he saw that there was a tall iron fence and an electric gate. And didn't guides have to have a license?

'Not here', he said quickly to the chauffeur. 'I made a mistake. I think it's the next one, or two or three doors further on.'

He decided on a large mansion set in an open lawn and stopping the chauffeur got out and walked up to the door. He was temporarily licked but at least he might bring back some story to soften them — say, that Miss Temple had mumps. He could point out her sick-room from the walk.

There was no answer to his ring but he saw that the door was partly ajar. Cautiously he pushed it open. He was staring into a deserted living-room on the baronial scale. He listened. There was no one about, no footsteps

in the first place: at the beginning

drugstore: pharmacy selling soft drinks □ **phone about it:** make the arrangements by phone
exchanged: used
pint: half a litre □ **swallows:** mouthfuls □ **behind:** hiding behind
after which: then
duck: abandon
with sound: talking
smackers: (slang) dollars □ **on the other hand:** but □ **might:** cf. may
on her way in or out: getting into the house or going out
Santa Anita: the Santa Anita horse races
glow: happy inner feeling □ **mounted:** returned

his spirit quailed: he panicked
tall: high □ **iron fence:** *grillage en fer*
gate: door □ **didn't guides have to:** were not guides obliged

further on: along the street
mansion: luxurious house □ **set:** situated □ **open:** without a fence □ **lawn:** *pelouse*
temporarily: for the moment □ **licked:** defeated □ **at least:** anyway
soften: pacify □ **say:** for example
mumps: *oreillons* □ **point out:** show □ **sick-room:** bedroom
walk: pavement

partly: a little □ **ajar:** open □ **cautiously:** carefully
staring: looking fixedly □ **on the baronial scale:** enormous
about: in the house □ **footsteps:** sound of someone walking

on the upper floor, no murmur from the kitchen. Pat took another pull at the gin. Then swiftly he hurried back to the limousine.

'She's at the studio,' he said quickly. 'But if we're quiet we can look at their living-room.'

Eagerly the Robinsons and Boojie disembarked and followed him. The living-room might have been Shirley Temple's, might have been one of many in Hollywood. Pat saw a doll in a corner and pointed at it, whereupon Mrs. Robinson picked it up, looked at it reverently and showed it to Boojie who sniffed indifferently.

'Could I meet Mrs. Temple?' she asked.

'Oh, she's out — nobody's home,' Pat said — unwisely.

'*No*body. Oh — then Boojie would so like a wee little peep at her bedroom.'

Before he could answer she had run up the stairs. Mr. Robinson followed and Pat waited uneasily in the hall, ready to depart at the sound either of an arrival outside or a commotion above.

He finished the bottle, disposed of it politely under a sofa cushion and then deciding that the visit upstairs was tempting fate too far, he went after his clients. On the stairs he heard Mrs. Robinson.

'But there's only *one* child's bedroom. I thought Shirley had brothers.'

A window on the winding staircase looked upon the street, and glancing out Pat saw a large car drive up to the curb. From it stepped a Hollywood celebrity who, though not one of those pursued by Mrs. Robinson was second to none in prestige and power. It was old Mr. Marcus, the

upper floor: first floor ☐ **took another pull at the gin:** he drank some gin from the bottle ☐ **swiftly:** quickly ☐ **hurried:** went quickly

quiet: not noisy, silent

eagerly: gladly, with pleasure ☐ **disembarked:** got out of the car
followed: went after ☐ **might:** could possibly
Shirley Temple's: Shirley Temple's house
doll: *poupée* ☐ **pointed at it:** showed it to the others
whereupon: at once ☐ **picked it up:** took it in her hands
reverently: respectfully ☐ **sniffed:** inhaled through the nose

Mrs. Temple: Shirley Temple's mother
nobody's home: nobody is at home ☐ **unwisely:** imprudently
so like: like so much ☐ **wee little:** very little, very quick
peep: furtive look

followed: went after her ☐ **uneasily:** uncomfortably
depart: run away ☐ **either... or:** *soit... soit* ☐ **arrival:** somebody coming in ☐ **commotion:** noise, disturbance ☐ **above:** upstairs
disposed of it: put it away

tempting fate too far: too risky ☐ **fate:** destiny
heard: cf. to hear
thought: cf. to think

winding: spiral ☐ **staircase:** stairs ☐ **looked upon:** opened on
glancing out: looking briefly outside ☐ **drive up:** arrive
curb: edge of pavement ☐ **from it stepped:** out of it emerged
though not one: though he was not one ☐ **second to none:** the best

producer, for whom Pat Hobby had been press agent twenty years ago.

At this point Pat lost his head. In a flash he pictured an elaborate explanation as to what he was doing here. He would not be forgiven. His occasional weeks in the studio at two-fifty would now disappear altogether and another finis would be written to his almost entirely finished career. He left, impetuously and swiftly — down the stairs, through the kitchen and out the back gate, leaving the Robinsons to their destiny.

Vaguely he was sorry for them as he walked quickly along the next boulevard. He could see Mr. Robinson producing his card as the head of Robdeer Food Products. He could see Mr. Marcus' skepticism, the arrival of the police, the frisking of Mr. and Mrs. Robinson.

Probably it would stop here — except that the Robinsons would be furious at him for his imposition. They would tell the police where they had picked him up.

Suddenly he went ricketing down the street, beads of gin breaking out profusely on his forehead. He had left his car beside Gus Venske's umbrella. And now he remembered another recognizing clue and hoped that Ronald Colman didn't know his last name.

press agent: in charge of relations with the press

lost his head: panicked □ **in a flash:** instantly □ **pictured:** imagined
elaborate: complicated □ **as to:** concerning
forgiven: cf. to forgive □ **occasional weeks:** infrequent jobs
two-fifty: 250 dollars a week □ **altogether:** completely
finis: end
left: ran away; to leave □ **impetuously:** with precipitation
out the back gate: out through the back gate □ **leaving... to their destiny:** abandoning

card: business card □ **head:** president
skepticism: doubts, suspicion
frisking: *fouille*
it would stop here: there would be no consequences
imposition: fraud, dishonesty
picked him up: found
ricketing: running feebly, like an old man □ **beads... breaking out:** perspiring □ **profusely:** abundantly □ **forehead:** *front*
beside: near
recognizing clue: proof of his identity
last name: family name, surname

Grammaire au fil des nouvelles

En traduisant les phrases suivantes au moyen des structures suggérées en italiques entre parenthèses essayez de retrouver le texte anglais dont la page et la ligne sont indiquées par des chiffres : le premier renvoie à la page, le second à la ligne.

Gus Venske n'était pas un excentrique et ses vêtements n'étaient pas non plus extraordinaires étant donné sa situation (*ni...ni,* 96.7).

Il lui fallut un moment pour comprendre (*traduction de falloir,* 98.12).

Pouvons-nous aller chez Robert Taylor et chez Clark Gable ? (*génitif,* 98.13).

Cela aurait été si facile dans le passé (*conditionnel passé,* 98.32).

Ceux qu'il avait le mieux connus étaient morts (*démonstratif,* 100.7).

Ils pourraient très bien être en train de tourner au studio (*auxiliaire de modalité,* 100.14).

Nous ferions mieux de prendre notre voiture (**had better**, 100.16).

À ce moment-là, la dame aurait oublié Gable (*conditionnel,* 100.28).

Nous connaissons une dame qui s'est fait photographier avec George Brent (*traduction de se faire + verbe,* 100.32).

Pourquoi faites-vous la grève ? (102.30).

Il vaudrait mieux que je voie comment les choses se présentent (104.13).

Il faudrait qu'il essaie Melvyn Douglas dont le bonjour était plus chaleureux que celui de Ronald Colman (*falloir ; traduction de dont ; génitif,* 104.32).

Je voulais vraiment monter voir leur chambre (**do** *emphatique,* 106.15).

NO HARM TRYING

Pat Hobby's apartment lay athwart a delicatessen shop on Wilshire Boulevard. And there lay Pat himself, surrounded by his books — the *Motion Picture Almanac* of 1928 and *Barton's Track Guide, 1939* — by his pictures, authentically signed photographs of Mabel Normand and Barbara LaMarr (who, being deceased, had no value in the pawn-shops) — and by his dogs in their cracked leather oxfords, perched on the arm of a slanting settee.

Pat was at "the end of his resources" — though this term is too ominous to describe a fairly usual condition in his life. He was an old-timer in pictures; he had once known sumptuous living, but for the past ten years jobs had been hard to hold — harder to hold than glasses.

"Think of it," he often mourned. "Only a writer — at forty-nine."

All this afternoon he had turned the pages of *The Times* and *The Examiner* for an idea. Though he did not intend to compose a motion picture from this idea, he needed it to get him inside a studio. If you had nothing to submit it was increasingly difficult to pass the gate. But though these two newspapers, together with *Life*, were the sources most commonly combed for "originals", they yielded him nothing this afternoon. There were wars, a fire in Topanga Canyon, press releases from the studios, municipal corruptions, and always the redeeming deeds of "The Trojuns", but Pat found nothing that competed in human interest with the betting page.

— If I could get out to Santa Anita, he thought — I could maybe get an idea about the nags.

This cheering idea was interrupted by his landlord, from the delicatessen store below.

"I told you I wouldn't deliver any more messages," said

lay athwart: was situated across ☐ **delicatessen shop:** *charcuterie*
Wilshire Boulevard: in Hollywood
surrounded by his books: with his books around him ☐ **motion picture:** film ☐ **track guide:** book on horses races
Mabel Normand... Barbara LaMarr: American actresses in silent films ☐ **deceased:** dead ☐ **pawn-shops:** places where money is lent on the security of personal property ☐ **dogs:** feet (slang)
leather oxfords: shoes ☐ **perched:** sitting ☐ **slanting:** inclined on one side ☐ **settee:** sofa ☐ **term:** word
ominous: pessimistic ☐ **fairly:** rather
old-timer: veteran ☐ **once:** in the past ☐ **known:** enjoyed
living: a way of life
hold: find and keep ☐ **glasses:** of alcohol
mourned: thought sadly, with regret ☐ **writer:** script-writer

though: *bien que* ☐ **intend:** want
it: this idea
submit: propose
increasingly: more and more ☐ **gate:** entrance door
***Life*:** illustrated weekly magazine
combed: prospected ☐ **originals:** scenarios ☐ **yielded:** produced
Topanga Canyon: district in Los Angeles
press releases: *communiqués*
redeeming: purifying ☐ **deeds:** adventures
competed: rivalled
betting page: the page on horse races
Santa Anita: where horse races are held
nags: horses
cheering: happy ☐ **landlord:** man who owns the apartment
below: under the apartment
deliver: give

Nick, "and *still* I won't. But Mr. Carl Le Vigne is telephoning in person from the studio and wants you should go over right away."

The prospect of a job did something to Pat. It anesthetized the crumbled, struggling remnants of his manhood, and inoculated him instead with a bland, easygoing confidence. The set speeches and attitudes of success returned to him. His manner as he winked at a studio policeman, stopped to chat with Louie, the bookie, and presented himself to Mr. Le Vigne's secretary, indicated that he had been engaged with momentous tasks in other parts of the globe. By saluting Le Vigne with a facetious "Hel-*lo* Captain!" he behaved almost as an equal, a trusted lieutenant who had never really been away.

"Pat, your wife's in the hospital", Le Vigne said. "It'll probably be in the papers this afternoon."

Pat started.

"My wife?" he said. "What wife?"

"Estelle. She tried to cut her wrists."

"Estelle!" Pat exclaimed. "You mean *Estelle*? Say, I was only married to her three weeks!"

"She was the best girl you ever had", said Le Vigne grimly.

"I haven't even heard of her for ten years."

"You're hearing about her now. They called all the studios trying to locate you."

"I had nothing to do with it."

"I know — she's only been here a week. She had a run of hard luck wherever it was she lived — New Orleans? Husband died, child died, no money..."

Pat breathed easier. They weren't trying to hang anything on him.

still I won't: I still don't want to
in person: himself □ **wants you should:** wants you to
right away: at once, immediately
prospect: chance □ **did:** changed □ **to:** in □ **anesthetized:** *anesthésiait* □ **crumbled:** decomposed □ **struggling:** fighting
remnants: rest □ **manhood:** dignity □ **instead:** *au lieu* □ **bland:** gentle
easygoing: indolent □ **confidence:** assurance □ **set:** stereotyped
manner: attitude □ **winked :** *fit un clin d'œil*
chat: talk □ **bookie:** man who takes money from people to bet on horses □ **presented himself:** gave his name
engaged: busy □ **momentous:** important □ **tasks:** jobs
the globe: the world □ **facetious:** humorous
behaved: acted □ **trusted:** reliable, responsible

papers: newspapers
started: made a gesture of surprise

cut her wrists: *s'ouvrir les veines*
say: but

grimly: severely
heard of her: had news about her

locate: find
I had nothing to do with it: it is not my fault
run of hard luck: a succession of misfortunes
wherever: in whatever place
died: cf. to die
easier: more easily □ **hang anything on him:** made him responsible for something

"Anyhow she'll live", Le Vigne reassured him superfluously, "— and she was the best script girl on the lot once. We'd like to take care of her. We thought the way was give you a job. Not exactly a job, because I know you're not up to it." He glanced into Pat's red-rimmed eyes. "More of a sinecure."

Pat became uneasy. He didn't recognize the word, but "sin" disturbed him and "cure" brought a whole flood of unpleasant memories.

"You're on the payroll at two-fifty a week for three weeks," said Le Vigne, "— but one-fifty of that goes to the hospital for your wife's bill."

"But we're divorced!" Pat protested. "No Mexican stuff either. I've been married since, and so has —"

"Take it or leave it. You can have an office here, and if anything you can do comes up we'll let you know."

"I never worked for a hundred a week."

"We're not asking you to work. If you want you can stay home."

Pat reversed his field.

"Oh, I'll work," he said quickly. "You dig me up a good story and I'll show you whether I can work or not."

Le Vigne wrote something on a slip of paper.

"All right. They'll find you an office."

Outside Pat looked at the memorandum.

"Mrs. John Devlin", it read, "Good Samaritan Hospital."

The very words irritated him.

"Good Samaritan!" he exclaimed. "Good gyp joint! One hundred and fifty bucks a week!"

anyhow: anyway ☐ **superfluously:** needlessly
script girl: assistant responsible for script ☐ **lot:** studio
the way: the best way to take care of her
give you a job: to give you a job
up to it: capable of doing it ☐ **glanced:** looked briefly ☐ **red-rimmed:** red ☐ **more of a:** something more like ☐ **sinecure:** easy job
uneasy: uncomfortable ☐ **recognize:** know
sin: *péché* ☐ **disturbed:** troubled ☐ **cure:** treatment ☐ **brought:** caused ☐ **a whole:** *tout un* ☐ **flood:** torrent, wave
on the payroll: employed ☐ **two-fifty:** 250 dollars ☐ **a week:** for a week ☐ **one-fifty:** 150 dollars ☐ **goes to:** will be for
for your wife's bill: to pay for her treatment
no Mexican stuff: not the kind of easy divorce you can get in Mexico
since: since that divorce ☐ **so has:** so has she
take it or leave it: *c'est à prendre ou à laisser*
if anything you can do comes up: if we find a job you can do ☐ **let you know:** tell you

reversed his field: changed his tactics
you dig me up: you find... for me
I'll show you: you will see if
slip: little piece

memorandum: the piece of paper

the very words: the words themselves
gyp: *escroquerie*
joint: (slang) place ☐ **bucks:** dollars

Pat had been given many a charity job but this was the first one that made him feel ashamed. He did not mind not *earning* his salary, but not getting it was another matter. And he wondered if other people on the lot who were obviously doing nothing, were being fairly paid for it. There were, for example, a number of beautiful young ladies who walked aloof as stars, and whom Pat took for stock girls, until Eric, the callboy, told him they were imports from Vienna and Budapest, not yet cast for pictures. Did half their pay checks go to keep husbands they had only had for three weeks!

The loveliest of these was Lizzette Starheim, a violet-eyed little blonde with an ill-concealed air of disillusion. Pat saw her alone at tea almost every afternoon in the commissary — and made her acquaintance one day by simply sliding into a chair opposite.

"Hello, Lizzette", he said. "I'm Pat Hobby, the writer."

"Oh, hel*lo*!"

She flashed such a dazzling smile that for a moment he thought she must have heard of him.

"When they going to cast you?" he demanded.

"I don't know." Her accent was faint and poignant.

"Don't let them give you the run-around. Not with a face like yours." Her beauty roused a rusty eloquence. "Sometimes they just keep you under contract till your teeth fall out, because you look too much like their big star."

"Oh no", she said distressfully.

"Oh yes!" he assured her. "I'm telling *you*. Why don't you go to another company and get borrowed? Have you thought of that idea?"

many a: lots of
ashamed: remorseful, guilty ☐ **mind:** object to
earning: meriting
another matter: not the same thing ☐ **wondered:** wanted to know
obviously: evidently ☐ **fairly:** equitably
a number of: many
aloof: distant ☐ **stock girls:** actresses hired by the studio for small parts ☐ **callboy:** attendant
imports: actresses who had come ☐ **cast:** who had not yet played in films ☐ **pay checks:** salaries ☐ **keep:** take care of, provide for

loveliest: most beautiful; sing. lovely ☐ **violet-eyed:** whose eyes were violet-colored ☐ **ill-concealed:** not well disguised, transparent
tea: tea-time
commissary: studio cafeteria ☐ **made her acquaintance:** got to know her ☐ **sliding:** *se glissant*

writer: script-writer

flashed... a smile: smiled widely ☐ **dazzling:** brilliant
have heard of him: know who he was
when they going: when are they going
faint: nearly imperceptible ☐ **poignant:** touching, moving
...run-around: make you wait
roused: awakened ☐ **rusty:** dissued, unpractised
keep you under contract: renew your contract to keep you ☐ **till:** until ☐ **your teeth fall out:** you are too old ☐ **look... like:** resemble
distressfully: with anguish

get borrowed: get another studio to employ you

"I think it's wonderful."

He intended to go further into the subject but Miss Starheim looked at her watch and got up.

"I must go now, Mr. —"

"Hobby. Pat Hobby."

Pat joined Dutch Waggoner, the director, who was shooting dice with a waitress at another table.

"Between pictures, Dutch?"

"Between pictures hell!" said Dutch. 'I haven't done a picture for six months and my contract's got six months to run. I'm trying to break it. Who was the little blonde?"

Afterwards, back in his office, Pat discussed these encounters with Eric the callboy.

"All signed up and no place to go", said Eric. "Look at this Jeff Manfred, now — an associate producer! Sits in his office and sends notes to the big shots — and I carry back word they're in Palm Springs. It breaks my heart. Yesterday he put his head on his desk and boohoo'd."

"What's the answer?" asked Pat.

"Changa management", suggested Eric, darkly. "Shake-up coming."

"Who's going to the top?" Pat asked, with scarcely concealed excitement.

"Nobody knows", said Eric. "But wouldn't I like to land uphill! Boy! I want a writer's job. I got three ideas so new they're wet behind the ears."

"It's no life at all", Pat assured him with conviction. "I'd trade with you right now."

In the hall next day he intercepted Jeff Manfred who

intended: wanted ☐ **go further into the subject:** continue talking
got up: stood up

joined: went to join ☐ **director:** who directs pictures
was shooting dice: *jouait aux dés* ☐ **waitress:** who serves customers
between pictures: when one film is finished and the next one has not begun yet ☐ **hell:** *au diable*
... six months to run: my contract will be over in 6 months
break: put an end to it

afterwards: later ☐ **back:** when he was back
encounters: meetings
all signed up: all those actresses and directors with contracts and no work to do ☐ **sits:** he sits
big shots: important people ☐ **I carry back word:** I have to answer that ☐ **Palm Springs:** holiday resort in California ☐ **breaks my heart:** makes me very sad
boohoo'd: cried
answer: solution
changa: a change of ☐ **management:** people who run the studio
darkly: sombrely ☐ **shake-up:** great changes
going to the top: going to be chief ☐ **scarcely:** little
concealed: dissimulated
wouldn't I like: I would be very happy
land uphill: get a better job than I have ☐ **boy:** God ☐ **I got:** I have got ☐ **ideas:** ideas for films ☐ **wet behind the ears:** like a newborn baby or animal ☐ **no life:** not a good life
trade: change, swap ☐ **right now:** at once

walked with the unconvincing hurry of one without a destination.

"What's the rush, Jeff?" Pat demanded, falling into step.

"Reading some scripts", Jeff panted without conviction.

Pat drew him unwillingly into his office.

"Jeff, have you heard about the shake-up?"

"Listen now, Pat —" Jeff looked nervously at the walls. "What shake-up?" he demanded.

"I heard that this Harmon Shaver is going to be the new boss", ventured Pat, "Wall Street control."

"Harmon Shaver!" Jeff scoffed. "He doesn't know anything about pictures — he's just a money man. He wanders around like a lost soul." Jeff sat back and considered. "Still — if you're *right*, he'd be a man you could get to." He turned mournful eyes on Pat. "I haven't been able to see Le Vigne or Barnes or Bill Behrer for a month. Can't get an assignment, can't get an actor, can't get a story." He broke off. "I've thought of drumming up something on my own. Got any ideas?"

"Have I?" said Pat. "I got three ideas so new they're wet behind the ears."

"Who for?"

"Lizzette Starheim", said Pat, "with Dutch Waggoner directing — see?"

"I'm with you all a hundred per cent," said Harmon Shaver. "This is the most encouraging experience I've had in pictures." He had a bright bond-salesman's chuckle. "By God, it reminds me of a circus, we got up when I was a boy."

with the unconvincing hurry: pretending he was in a hurry

what's the rush: why are you in a hurry □ **falling into step:** walking at the same speed
panted without conviction: pretending he was out of breath

drew him into: made him enter □ **unwillingly:** against his will
heard about: heard any news □ **shake-up:** change of management

... at the walls: Jeff did not want to be overheard

ventured: speculated □ **Wall Street:** New York financial district, also bankers and financiers □ **scoffed:** said with sarcasm
pictures: films
wanders around: walks around □ **lost soul:** *âme en peine*
still: but, on the other hand □ **he'd be:** he would be
get to: get access to, manage to talk to □ **mournful:** sad

can't get: I can't get □ **an assignment:** a film to make
broke off: interrupted himself
drumming up: inventing, writing □ **on my own:** alone
have I: of course I have □ **I got:** I have got

who for: who are they for

directing: being the director of the film

I'm with you: I agree with you

bright: cheerful □ **bond:** *obligation* □ **chuckle:** suppressed laughter
reminds: makes me think □ **got up:** set up, created

They had come to his office inconspicuously like conspirators — Jeff Manfred, Waggoner, Miss Starheim and Pat Hobby.

"You like the idea, Miss Starheim?" Shaver continued.

"I think it's wonderful."

"And you, Mr. Waggoner?"

"I've heard only the general line", said Waggoner with director's caution, "but it seems to have the old emotional socko." He winked at Pat. "I didn't know this old tramp had it in him."

Pat glowed with pride. Jeff Manfred, though he was elated, was less sanguine.

"It's important nobody talks", he said nervously. "The Big Boys would find some way of killing it. In a week, when we've got the script done we'll go to them."

"I agree," said Shaver. "They have run the studio so long that — well, I don't trust my own secretaries — I sent them to the races this afternoon."

Back in Pat's office Eric, the callboy, was waiting. He did not know that he was the hinge upon which swung a great affair.

"You like the stuff, eh?" he asked eagerly.

"Pretty good", said Pat with calculated indifference.

"You said you'd pay more for the next batch."

"Have a heart!" Pat was aggrieved. "How many callboys get seventy-five a week?"

"How many callboys can write?"

Pat considered. Out of the two hundred a week Jeff Manfred was advancing from his own pocket, he had naturally awarded himself a commission of sixty per cent.

"I'll make it a hundred," he said. "Now check yourself off the lot and meet me in front of Benny's bar."

inconspicuously: secretly

the general line: the general idea
caution: prudence
socko: force, strength, punch ☐ **winked:** *fit un clin d'œil* ☐ **tramp:** vagabond ☐ **had it in him:** could still work so well
glowed: was full of ☐ **pride:** pleasure
elated: pleased, proud ☐ **sanguine:** hopeful, confident
nobody talks: nobody should talk
Big Boys: the bosses ☐ **killing:** put an end to
done: written, finished ☐ **go to them:** show them the script
run: managed, been the bosses
trust my... secretaries: think my secretaries are loyal
races: horse races

hinge: central character ☐ **upon which swung a great affair:** an important business depended on
stuff: what I have written ☐ **eargerly:** with impatience
pretty: rather
you'd pay: you would pay ☐ **batch:** series, lot
have a heart: show some compassion ☐ **aggrieved:** hurt
seventy-five: seventy-five dollars

considered: reflected ☐ **out of:** *sur*

awarded himself: allocated himself
I'll make it: I'll raise it to ☐ **check yourself off the lot:** leave the studio

At the hospital, Estelle Hobby Devlin sat up in bed, overwhelmed by the unexpected visit.

"I'm glad you came, Pat", she said, "you've been very kind. Did you get my note?"

"Forget it," Pat said gruffly. He had never liked this wife. She had loved him too much — until she found suddenly that he was a poor lover. In her presence he felt inferior.

"I got a guy outside", he said.

"What for?"

"I thought maybe you had nothing to do and you might want to pay me back for all this jack —"

He waved his hand around the bare hospital room.

"You were a swell script girl once. Do you think if I got a typewriter you could put some good stuff into continuity?"

"Why — yes. I suppose I could."

"It's a secret. We can't trust anybody at the studio."

"All right", she said.

"I'll send this kid in with the stuff. I got a conference."

"All right — and — oh Pat — come and see me again."

"Sure, I'll come."

But he knew he wouldn't. He didn't like sickrooms — he lived in one himself. From now on he was done with poverty and failure. He admired strength — he was taking Lizzette Starheim to a wrestling match that night.

In his private musings Harmon Shaver referred to the showdown as "the surprise party." He was going to confront Le Vigne with a *fait accompli* and he gathered his

sat up: was sitting
overwhelmed: impressed □ **unexpected:** which she didn't expect

note: short letter
forget it: don't mention it □ **gruffly:** ungraciously
until: *jusqu'à ce que*
a poor lover: not a good lover

I got a guy: I brought a man □ **outside:** waiting outside
what for: why

jack: (slang) money, cost, expenses
waved his hands around: pointed to, indicated □ **bare:** simple
swell: super □ **script-girl:** who records information about the photographing of each scene □ **typewriter:** *machine à écrire*
continuity: a complete scenario

kid: young boy □ **send... in:** send him to you □ **got:** have got

wouldn't: wouldn't come □ **sickrooms:** rooms in which people are confined by sickness □ **done with:** finished with
failure: lack of success; to fail □ **strength:** force, energy
wrestling: *lutte*

musings: reflections, dreams
showdown: crisis
gathered: brought together

coterie before phoning Le Vigne to come over to his office.

"What for?" demanded Le Vigne. "Couldn't you tell me now — I'm busy as hell."

This arrogance irritated Shaver — who was here to watch over the interests of Eastern stockholders.

"I don't ask much", he said sharply, "I let you fellows laugh at me behind my back and freeze me out of things. But now I've got something and I'd like you to come over."

"All right — all right."

Le Vigne's eyebrows lifted as he saw the members of the new production unit but he said nothing — sprawled into an arm chair with his eyes on the floor and his fingers over his mouth.

Mr. Shaver came around the desk and poured forth words that had been fermenting in him for months. Simmered to its essentials, his protest was: "You would not let me play, but I'm going to play anyhow." Then he nodded to Jeff Manfred — who opened the script and read aloud. This took an hour, and still Le Vigne sat motionless and silent.

"There you are," said Shaver triumphantly. "Unless you've got any objection I think we ought to assign a budget to this proposition and get going. I'll answer to my people."

Le Vigne spoke at last.

"You like it, Miss Starheim?"

"I think it's wonderful."

"What language you going to play it in?"

To everyone's surprise Miss Starheim got to her feet.

coterie: group of people

what for: why
busy as hell: extremely busy
watch over the interests: take care of the interests
Eastern: on the East Coast □ **stockholders:** *actionnaires*
sharply: severely □ **fellows:** men, guys
freeze me out of things: exclude me

eyebrows: *sourcils* □ **lifted:** went up □ **as:** when
unit: group □ **sprawled:** spread himself

poured forth: discharged, released; cf. to pour water
had been fermenting in him: had agitated him
simmered: reduced
would not: did not want to □ **play:** produce films
nodded: inclined head in command
took: cf. to take □ **still:** all the time
motionless: not moving
unless you've got any objection: if you have no objection
ought to: should □ **assign:** allocate
get going: start filming □ **I'll answer to my people:** I will make sure the people I work for agree
at last: finally

you going: are you going
got to her feet: stood up

"I must go now," she said with her faint poignant accent.

"Sit down and answer me", said Le Vigne. "What language are you playing it in?"

Miss Starheim looked tearful.

"Wenn I gute teachers hätte konnte ich dann thees rôle gut spielen", she faltered.

"But you like the script."

She hesitated.

"I think it's wonderful."

Le Vigne turned to the others.

"Miss Starheim has been here eight months", he said. "She's had three teachers. Unless things have changed in the past two weeks she can say just three sentences. She can say, 'How do you do'; she can say, 'I think it's wonderful'; and she can say, 'I must go now.' Miss Starheim has turned out to be a pinhead — I'm not insulting her because she doesn't know what it means. Anyhow — there's your Star."

He turned to Dutch Waggoner, but Dutch was already on his feet.

"Now Carl —" he said defensively.

"You force me to it", said Le Vigne. "I've trusted drunks up to a point, but I'll be goddam if I'll trust a hophead."

He turned to Harmon Shaver.

"Dutch has been good for exactly one week apiece on his last four pictures. He's all right now but as soon as the heat goes on he reaches for the little white powders. Now Dutch! Don't say anything you'll regret. We're carrying you in *hopes* — but you won't get on a stage till we've had a doctor's certificate for a year."

faint: almost imperceptible ☐ **poignant:** sad, touching

what language... in: what language are you going to use in the film
tearful: she had tears in her eyes
wenn... spielen: when I have good teachers, I will be able to play this part well ☐ **faltered:** said hesitantly

turned to: looked at
here: in Hollywood
she's had: she has had ☐ **unless:** *à moins que*
past: last

turned out to be: been found to be ☐ **pinhead:** fool, idiot
I'm not insulting her: the word is not insulting
anyhow: anyway, in one way or another
already: at once, immediately
on his feet: standing

trusted drunks: had confidence in people who drink too much
up to a point: a little ☐ **goddam:** damned
a hophead: someone who uses drugs, an addict

has been good: has worked correctly ☐ **apiece:** each time
all right: not taking drugs ☐ **as soon as:** *dès que* ☐ **the heat goes on:** things get more difficult ☐ **reaches for... powders:** uses drugs
carrying you: keeping you in the company
get on a stage: get a job as a director ☐ **till:** until
for a year: saying that you have not taken drugs for a year

Again he turned to Harmon.

"There's your director. Your supervisor, Jeff Manfred, is here for one reason only — because he's Behrer's wife's cousin. There's nothing against him but he belongs to silent days as much as — as much as —" His eyes fell upon a quavering broken man, "— as much as Pat Hobby."

"What do you mean?" demanded Jeff.

"You trusted Hobby, didn't you? That tells the whole story." He turned back to Shaver. "Jeff's a weeper and a wisher and a dreamer. Mr. Shaver, you have bought a lot of condemned building material."

"Well, I've bought a good story", said Shaver defiantly.

"Yes. That's right. We'll make that story."

"Isn't that something?" demanded Shaver. "With all this secrecy how was I to know about Mr. Waggoner and Miss Starheim? But I do know a good story."

"Yes", said Le Vigne absently. He got up. "Yes — it's a good story... Come along to my office, Pat."

He was already at the door. Pat cast an agonized look at Mr. Shaver as if for support. Then, weakly, he followed.

"Sit down, Pat."

"That Eric's got talent, hasn't he?" said Le Vigne. "He'll go places. How'd you come to dig him up?"

Pat felt the straps of the electric chair being adjusted.

"Oh — I just dug him up. He — came in my office."

"We're putting him on salary", said Le Vigne. "We ought to have some system to give these kids a chance."

He took a call on his Dictograph, then swung back to Pat.

there's your director: this is the director you wanted
Behrer's wife's cousin: a cousin of the wife of one of the bosses
against him: to say against him □ **belongs to silent days:** he can only do silent pictures □ **his eyes fell upon:** he looked at
quavering: trembling with fear

didn't you: *non* □ **tells the whole story:** is revealing
turned back to: looked again at □ **weeper:** someone who always complains □ **... wisher... dreamer:** who never manages to do anything □ **a lot of... material:** men who are good for nothing

defiantly: agressively, with insolence
make that story: make that film

secrecy: secrets □ **how was I to know:** how could I possibly guess
I do know: there's no doubt I can recognize

come along: come with me
cast... a look: looked at □ **agonized:** unhappy, frightened
as is for: as if he wanted □ **weakly:** obediently
followed: went out with Le Vigne

Eric's got: Eric has got
go places: go far □ **how'd you come:** how did you manage
dig him up: find him
straps: *lanières*
dug: cf. to dig
putting him on salary: giving him a job
kids: young people
took a call: answered a telephone call □ **swung back:** turned to Pat; cf. to swing (on a revolving armchair)

"But how did you ever get mixed up with this goddam Shaver. *You*, Pat — an old-timer like you."

"Well, I thought —"

"Why doesn't he go back East?" continued Le Vigne disgustedly. "Getting all you poops stirred up!"

Blood flowed back into Pat's veins. He recognized his signal, his dog-call.

"Well, I got you a story, didn't I?" he said, with almost a swagger. And he added, "How'd you know about it?"

"I went down to see Estelle in the hospital. She and this kid were working on it. I walked right in on them."

"Oh", said Pat.

"I knew the kid by sight. Now, Pat, tell me this — did Jeff Manfred think you wrote it — or was he in on the racket?"

"Oh God", Pat mourned. "What do I have to answer that for?"

Le Vigne leaned forward intensely.

"Pat, you're sitting over a trap door!" he said with savage eyes. "Do you see how the carpet's cut? I just have to press this button and drop you down to hell! Will you *talk*?"

Pat was on his feet, staring wildly at the floor.

"Sure I will!" he cried. He believed it — he believed such things.

"All right", said Le Vigne relaxing. "There's whiskey in the sideboard there. Talk quick and I'll give you another month at two-fifty. I kinda like having you around."

get mixed up: get involved □ **goddam:** *foutu*
old-timer: veteran

back East: back to New York
disgustedly: expressing repugnance □ **poops:** stupid people □ **stirred up:** excited □ **blood:** *sang* □ **flowed back:** started running again □ **dog-call:** the call a dog answers

a swagger: self-satisfaction □ **how'd you:** how did you

walked right in on them: surprised them

I knew the kid by sight: I had seen him in the studio
was he in on the racket: did he know of the trick

mourned: said unhappily □ **what... for:** why

leaned forward: inclined his body forward over the desk

how the carpet's cut: how the carpet is cut
drop you: make you fall □ **hell:** *enfer*

was on his feet: stood up □ **staring wildly:** looking fixedly

sideboard: *buffet* □ **quick:** quickly
two-fifty: 250 dollars □ **kinda:** kind of □ **around:** in the studio

Grammaire au fil des nouvelles

En traduisant les phrases suivantes au moyen des structures suggérées en italiques entre parenthèses essayez de retrouver le texte anglais dont la page et la ligne sont indiquées par des chiffres : le premier renvoie à la page, le second à la ligne.

Trouve-moi une bonne histoire et tu verras si, oui ou non, je peux travailler (**whether**, 120.21).

Ne pas mériter son salaire ne le gênait pas mais ne pas le toucher, c'était une autre histoire (**to mind** + *gérondif*, 122.2).

Il se demanda si d'autres que lui étaient payés à ne rien faire (*passif ; forme en* **-ing**, 122.4).

La plus jolie d'entre elles était une petite blonde aux yeux violets (*superlatif ; adjectif composé*, 122.12).

Un moment, il crut qu'elle avait dû entendre parler de lui (*modalité*, 122.20).

Un emploi d'écrivain (*génitif générique*, 124.27).

Il ignore tout du cinéma (**not...any**, 126.13).

Cela me rappelle un cirque que nous avions monté quand j'étais enfant (**to remind**, 126.31).

Il ne savait pas qu'il était le pivot sur lequel reposait toute l'affaire ((*relative*, 128.20).

Reviens me voir. — Bien sûr que je reviendrai. Mais il savait qu'il ne reviendrait pas (*reprise de l'auxiliaire*, 130.21,22,23).

Vous n'avez pas voulu me laisser jouer mais je vais jouer quand même (**would ; let**, 132.18,19).

Comment pouvais-je savoir ? (**to be to**, 136.16).

A PATRIOTIC SHORT

Pat Hobby, the writer and the man, had his great success in Hollywood during what Irvin Cobb refers to as 'the mosaic swimming-pool age — just before the era when they had to have a shinbone of St Sebastian for a clutch lever.'

Mr. Cobb no doubt exaggerates, for when Pat had his pool in those fat days of silent pictures, it was entirely cement, unless you should count the cracks where the water stubbornly sought its own level through the mud.

'But it *was* a pool,' he assured himself one afternoon more than a decade later. Though he was now more than grateful for this small chore he had assigned him by producer Berners — one week at two-fifty — all the insolence of office could not take that memory away.

He had been called in to the studio to work upon an humble short. It was based on the career of General Fitzhugh Lee who fought for the Confederacy and later for the U.S.A. against Spain — so it would offend neither North nor South. And in the recent conference Pat had tried to cooperate.

'I was thinking —' he suggested to Jack Berners '— that it might be a good thing if we could give it a Jewish touch.'

'What do you mean?' demanded Jack Berners quickly.

'Well I thought — the way things are and all, it would be a sort of good thing to show that there were a number of Jews in it too.'

'In what?'

'In the Civil War.' Quickly he reviewed his meager history. 'They were, weren't they?'

'Naturally,' said Berners, with some impatience, 'I suppose everybody was except the Quakers.'

'Well, my idea was that we could have this Fitzhugh Lee

writer: script writer
what... refers to: the period Irvin Cobb describes as
mosaic swimming-pool: *piscine en mosaïque* ☐ **era:** period
shinbone: tibia ☐ **clutch lever:** *manette d'embrayage*
no doubt: certainly ☐ **for:** because
fat: prosperous ☐ **pictures:** films
unless: except if ☐ **cracks:** fissures
stubbornly: tenaciously ☐ **sought:** followed ☐ **mud:** *boue*
pool: swimming-pool
decade: period of ten years ☐ **though:** but
grateful: thankful ☐ **chore:** job, task ☐ **he had assigned him:** he had been given ☐ **two-fifty:** 250 dollars ☐ **insolence of office:** the self assurance the job gave him ☐ **take away:** destroy
called in to: asked to come ☐ **upon:** on
humble: unimportant ☐ **short:** short film or documentary
fought: to fight, fought, fought ☐ **Confederacy:** the Southern states which seceded from the U.S.A. in 1860 ☐ **offend:** give offence
neither... nor: *ni... ni* ☐ **conference:** meeting
tried: to try

might: cf. may, might ☐ **Jewish:** adj. *juif*; a Jew

the way things are and all: in the situation we are in

reviewed: tried to remember ☐ **his meager history:** the little knowledge he had of history

Quakers: religious group known for its pacifism

in love with a Jewish girl. He's going to be shot at curfew so she grabs a church bell—'

Jack Berners leaned forward earnestly.

'Say, Pat, you want this job, don't you? Well, I told you the story. You got the first script. If you thought up this tripe to please me you're losing your grip.'

Was that a way to treat a man who had once owned a pool which had been talked about by —

That was how he happened to be thinking about his long lost swimming-pool as he entered the shorts department. He was remembering a certain day over a decade ago in all its details, how he had arrived at the studio in his car driven by a Filipino in uniform; the deferential bow of the guard at the gate which had admitted car and all to the lot, his ascent to that long lost office which had a room for the secretary and was really a director's office...

His reverie was broken off by the voice of Ben Brown, head of the shorts department, who walked him into his own chambers.

'Jack Berners just phoned me,' he said. 'We don't want any new angles, Pat. We've got a good story. Fitzhugh Lee was a dashing cavalry commander. He was a nephew of Robert E. Lee and we want to show him at Appomattox, pretty bitter and all that. And then show how he became reconciled — we'll have to be careful because Virginia is swarming with Lees — and how he finally accepts a U.S. commission from President McKinley —'

Pat's mind darted back again into the past. The President — that was the magic word that had gone around that morning many years ago. The President of the United States was going to make a visit to the

shot: killed by rifle; to shoot, shot, shot □ **curfew:** *couvre-feu*
grabs: seizes □ **bell:** *cloche*
leaned forward: inclined his body □ **earnestly:** seriously
told: to tell, told, told
got: received □ **thought up:** imagined
tripe: nonsense □ **grip:** aptitude, ability
once: in the past □ **owned:** possessed

happened to be: came to be □ **long lost:** lost long ago
shorts: short films

deferential: respectful □ **bow:** salutation
car and all: the car and its occupants
lot: studio □ **his ascent to:** the walk to
director: who directs films
broken off: to break, broke, broken
head: chief, boss □ **walked him:** walked with him
chambers: office

new angles: new ideas
dashing: splendid □ **Robert E. Lee:** (1807-1870) general who commanded the Confederate armies in the American Civil War and surrendered in Appomattox in 1865 □ **pretty bitter:** very angry, hurt, acrimonious □ **reconciled:** resigned
Virginia is swarming with Lees: there are many people called Lee in Virginia □ **commission:** command given to an officer
McKinley: William McKinley (1843-1901) 20th President
mind: spirit □ **darted back:** went quickly back

lot. Everyone had been agog about it — it seemed to mark a new era in pictures because a President of the United States had never visited a studio before. The executives of the company were all dressed up — from a window of his long lost Beverly Hills house Pat had seen Mr. Maranda, whose mansion was next door to him, bustle down his walk in a cutaway coat at nine o'clock, and had known that something was up. He thought maybe it was clergy but when he reached the lot he had found it was the President of the United States himself who was coming...

'Clean up the stuff about Spain,' Ben Brown was saying. 'The guy that wrote it was a Red and he's got all the Spanish officers with ants in their pants. Fix up that.'

In the office assigned him Pat looked at the script of *True to Two Flags*. The first scene showed General Fitzhugh Lee at the head of his cavalry receiving word that Petersburg had been evacuated. In the script Lee took the blow in pantomime, but Pat was getting two-fifty a week — so, casually and without effort, he wrote in one of his favorite lines:

Lee (to his officers)

Well, what are you standing here gawking for? DO something!

6. Medium Shot Officers pepping up, slapping each other on back, etc.

Dissolve to:

To what? Pat's mind dissolved once more into the glamorous past. On that happy day in the twenties his

agog: in suspense, expectant ☐ **it:** the visit
era: period ☐ **pictures:** films
executives: managers, heads of departments
dressed up: dressed in their best clothes
Beverly Hills: elegant district of Los Angeles
mansion: large residence ☐ **next door:** near ☐ **bustle down:** hurry down ☐ **cutaway coat:** *queue de pie*
something was up: something was going to happen ☐ **clergy:** members of religious orders ☐ **reached:** arrived at ☐ **lot:** studio

clean up: change ☐ **stuff:** text
guy: man ☐ **wrote:** to write, wrote, written ☐ **Red:** Communist
ants in their pants: being nervous ☐ **fix up:** arrange

assigned him: that had been given to him ☐ **true:** faithful
flags: *drapeaux*
head: forefront, front line ☐ **word:** news
Petersburg: city in southern Virginia where a major battle of the Civil War was fought in 1864-1865 ☐ **blow:** bad news
casually: in a relaxed manner ☐ **wrote in:** added
lines: lines of dialogue

what... for: why ☐ **gawking:** looking fixedly with eyes wide open

medium shot: *plan moyen* ☐ **pepping up:** reviving ☐ **slapping:** striking
dissolve: fade; *fondu*

dissolved: lost itself ☐ **once more:** another time
glamorous: exciting, prestigious ☐ **twenties:** the 1920s

phone had rung at about noon. It had been Mr. Maranda.

'Pat, the President is lunching in the private dining room. Doug Fairbanks can't come so there's a place empty and anyhow we think there ought to be one writer there.'

His memory of the luncheon was palpitant with glamour. The Great Man had asked some questions about pictures and had told a joke and Pat laughed and laughed with the others — all of them solid men together — rich, happy and successful.

Afterwards the President was to go on some sets and see somes scenes taken and still later he was going to Mr. Maranda's house to meet some of the women stars at tea. Pat was not invited to that party but he went home early anyhow and from his veranda saw the cortège drive up, with Mr. Maranda beside the President in the back seat. Ah he was proud of pictures then — of his position in them — of the President of the happy country where he was born...

Returning to reality Pat looked down at the script of *True to Two Flags* and wrote slowly and thoughtfully: *Insert: A calendar — with the years plainly marked and the sheets blowing off in a cold wind, to show Fitzhugh Lee growing older and older.*

His labors had made him thirsty — not for water, but he knew better than to take anything else his first day on the job. He got up and went out into the hall and along the corridor to the water-cooler.

As he walked he slipped back into his reverie.

That had been a lovely California afternoon so Mr. Maranda had taken his exalted guest and the coterie of stars

rung: to ring, rang, rung □ **noon:** midday

lunching: having lunch □ **private:** not open to the public
Doug Fairbanks: (1883-1939) famous US film actor
anyhow: in any case □ **ought to be:** should be □ **writer:** script-writer

luncheon: lunch □ **palpitant:** ecstatic, enthusiastic
glamour: prestige, magic, splendour □ **Great Man:** President
told: to tell, told, told □ **joke:** funny story
solid men: important men

afterwards: later □ **was to:** had planned □ **sets:** *plateaux*
some scenes taken: some scenes being filmed □ **still:** *encore*
women stars: actresses

early: sooner than usual □ **anyhow:** in any case □ **cortège:** the President and his entourage □ **drive up:** arrive □ **beside:** sitting near
seat: cf. to sit, sat, sat □ **was proud:** had a high opinion □ **then:** at that time

script: scenario
thoughtfully: with concentration □ **insert:** new shot to be introduced □ **plainly:** clearly □ **sheets:** *feuilles*
blowing off: flying off like leaves □ **growing:** getting

labors: work □ **...thirsty:** he wanted a drink; to be thirsty for
knew better than: knew it was not correct □ **anything else:** any other drink □ **got up:** stood up; to get, got, got
water-cooler: container of artificially cooled drinking water
as: while □ **slipped back:** went back, relapsed
lovely: splendid
exalted: prestigious □ **guest:** *invité* □ **coterie:** circle

into his garden, which adjoined Pat's garden. Pat had gone out his back door and followed a low privet hedge keeping out of sight — and then accidentally come face to face with the Presidential party.

The President had smiled and nodded. Mr. Maranda smiled and nodded.

'You met Mr. Hobby at lunch,' Mr. Maranda said to the President. 'He's one of our writers.'

'Oh yes,' said the President, 'you write the pictures.'

'Yes I do,' said Pat.

The President glanced over into Pat's property.

'I suppose —' he said, '— that you get lots of inspiration sitting by the side of that fine pool.'

'Yes,' said Pat, 'yes, I do.'

... Pat filled his cup at the cooler. Down the hall there was a group approaching — Jack Berners, Ben Brown and several other executives and with them a girl to whom they were very attentive and deferential. He recognized her face — she was the girl of the year, the It girl, the Oomph girl, the Glamour Girl, the girl for whose services every studio was in violent competition.

Pat lingered over his drink. He had seen many phonies break in and break out again, but this girl was the real thing, someone to stir every pulse in the nation. He felt his own heart beat faster. Finally, as the procession drew near, he put down the cup, dabbed at his hair with his hand and took a step out into the corridor.

The girl looked at him — he looked at the girl. Then she took one arm of Jack Berners' and one of Ben Brown's and suddenly the party seemed to walk right through him — so that he had to take a step back against the wall.

An instant later Jack Berners turned around and said

adjoined: was contiguous with
gone out: gone out of □ **followed:** went along □ **privet hedge:** *haie de troènes* □ **out of sight:** invisible □ **come face to face:** meet
party: circle, group

nodded: inclined his head as a sign of salutation
met: to meet, met, met

glanced over: gave a brief look over the hedge □ **property:** house and garden □ **get:** obtain, come across
by the side: near □ **fine:** beautiful

filled: cf. full □ **down the hall:** at the other end of the hall

several: a few □ **whom:** cf. who

It girl... Oomph girl... Glamour Girl: Hollywood terms first used in the 1930s to describe girls full of sex appeal and gaiety
...in violent competition: all the studios wanted to engage her
lingered: took his time □ **phonies:** impostors, fakes
break in: appear □ **break out:** disappear □ **the real thing:** authentic
stir every pulse in: electrify, impassion
heart: *cœur* □ **drew near:** came nearer
dabbed his hair: touched, arranged □ **took a step:** advanced

party: group □ **right through him:** as if he wasn't there
take a step back: retreat
turned around: looked back

back to him, 'Hello, Pat.' And then some of the others threw half glances around but no one else spoke, so interested were they in the girl.

In his office, Pat looked at the scene where President McKinley offers a United States commission to Fitzhugh Lee. Suddenly he gritted his teeth and bore down on his pencil as he wrote:

Lee

Mr. President, you can take your commission and go straight to hell.

Then he bent down over his desk, his shoulders shaking as he thought of that happy day when he had had a swimming-pool.

threw half glances around: turned around to look at him briefly; to throw ☐ **so interested were they:** because they were so interested

gritted his teeth: *serra les dents* ☐ **bore down on:** applied force, pushed strongly

straight: directly, immediately ☐ **to hell:** to the devil

bent down: inclined his body downward ☐ **shaking:** trembling
as: when

Grammaire au fil des nouvelles

En traduisant les phrases suivantes au moyen des structures suggérées en italiques entre parenthèses essayez de retrouver le texte anglais dont la page et la ligne sont indiquées par des chiffres : le premier renvoie à la page, le second à la ligne.

On l'avait appelé au studio pour travailler sur un humble court métrage (*passif,* 142.14).

Etait-ce une façon de traiter un homme qui avait autrefois possédé une piscine qui avait été remarquée par le Président ? (*relatives,* 144.7).

C'était ainsi qu'il en était venu à penser à sa piscine depuis longtemps perdue (**to happen** ; *adjectif composé,* 144.9).

Dans le bureau qu'on lui avait attribué, Pat regarda le manuscrit (*passif,* 146.15).

Le Président devait ensuite se rendre sur quelques plateaux pour voir tourner quelques scènes (*to be to ; to see + verbe,* 148.12).

Ses efforts lui avaient donné soif (*causatif,* 148.26).

De sa fenêtre, il vit le cortège arriver (**to see** + *verbe,* 148.16)).

En marchant, il retourna à sa rêverie (*traduction de en + participe présent,* 148.30).

Il y avait avec eux une fille envers laquelle ils faisaient preuve de beaucoup de déférence (*relative,* 150.17).

Ils étaient si intéressés par la fille que personne ne parla à Pat. (*inversion,* 152.3).

ON THE TRAIL OF PAT HOBBY

The day was dark from the outset, and a California fog crept everywhere. It had followed Pat in his headlong, hatless flight across the city. His destination, his refuge, was the studio, where he was not employed but which had been home to him for twenty years.

Was it his imagination or did the policeman at the gate give him and his pass an especially long look? It might be the lack of a hat — Hollywood was full of hatless men but Pat felt marked, especially as there had been no opportunity to part his thin grey hair.

In the writers' building he went into the lavatory. Then he remembered: by some inspired ukase from above, all mirrors had been removed from the writers' building a year ago.

Across the hall he saw Bee McIlvaine's door ajar, and discerned her plump person.

'Bee, can you loan me your compact box?' he asked.

Bee looked at him suspiciously, then frowned and dug it from her purse.

'You on the lot?' she inquired.

'Will be next week', he prophesied. He put the compact on her desk and bent over it with his comb. 'Why won't they put mirrors back in the johnnies? Do they think writers would look at themselves all day?'

'Remember when they took out the couches?' said Bee. 'In nineteen thirty-two. And they put them back in thirty-four.'

'I worked at home', said Pat feelingly.

Finished with her mirror he wondered if she were good for a loan — enough to buy a hat or something to eat. Bee must have seen the look in his eyes for she forestalled him.

'The Finns got all my money', she said, 'and I'm worried

dark: sombre ☐ **outset:** beginning ☐ **fog:** *brouillard*
crept: insinuated itself ☐ **it:** the fog ☐ **headlong:** desperate
hatless: without a hat ☐ **flight:** escape; cf. to flee
studio: Hollywood cinema studio
home to him: like a home to him
gate: door, entrance of the studio
give... a look: examine ☐ **pass:** entrance permit
the lack of a hat: Pat had no hat on
marked: the object of suspicion ☐ **no opportunity:** no time, no occasion ☐ **to part:** to comb, to arrange ☐ **thin:** not abundant
lavatory: toilet ☐ **then:** at that moment
by: because of, due to ☐ **ukase:** order ☐ **from above:** from the studio manager ☐ **removed:** taken out; cf. a removal

across: on the other side of ☐ **ajar:** slightly open
discerned: could see ☐ **plump:** corpulent
loan: let me use ☐ **compact box:** small box for face powder
frowned: *fronça les sourcils* ☐ **dug it from:** took it out of cf. to dig
purse: small woman's handbag
lot: studio area ☐ **on the lot:** employed by the studio
will be: I will be ☐ **prophesied:** predicted
bent over it: inclined his head over it ☐ **why won't they:** why are they determined not to ☐ **johnnies:** toilet, lavatory; cf. the john

couches: sofas

feelingly: with emotion
finished with: having finished ☐ **wondered:** tried to guess
good for a loan: ready to give him a little money that he would give her back later ☐ **look:** expression ☐ **forestalled:** anticipated
Finns: inhabitants of Finland (invaded by Russia in 1939)

about my job. Either my picture starts tomorrow or it's going to be shelved. We haven't even got a title.'

She handled him a mimeographed bulletin from the scenario department and Pat glanced at the headline.

TO ALL DEPARTMENTS

TITLE WANTED — FIFTY DOLLARS REWARD

SUMMARY FOLLOWS

'I could use fifty', Pat said. 'What's it about?'

'It's written there. It's about a lot of stuff that goes on in tourist cabins.'

Pat started and looked at her wild-eyed. He had thought to be safe here behind the guarded gates but news traveled fast. This was a friendly or perhaps not so friendly warning. He must move on. He was a hunted man now, with nowhere to lay his hatless head.

'I don't know anything about that', he mumbled and walked hastily from the room.

II

Just inside the door of the commissary Pat looked around. There was no guardian except the girl at the cigarette stand but obtaining another person's hat was subject to one complication: it was hard to judge the size by a cursory glance, while the sight of a man trying on several hats in a check room was unavoidably suspicious.

Personal taste also obtruded itself. Pat was beguiled by a green fedora with a sprightly feather but it was too readily identifiable. This was also true of a fine white Stetson for

either... or: *soit... soit* ☐ **starts:** begins
shelved: abandoned ☐ **title:** name
handled him: gave him; cf. hand ☐ **mimeographed bulletin:** a copy of the bulletin ☐ **glanced:** looked ☐ **headline:** line at top of the page

title wanted: a title is needed ☐ **reward:** recompense
summary: *résumé* ☐ **follows:** comes after

fifty: fifty dollars
written: to write, wrote, written ☐ **stuff:** stories ☐ **goes on:** happens
tourist cabins: holiday bungalows
started: made a sudden movement from surprise ☐ **wild-eyed:** with a mad look ☐ **safe... behind the... gates:** protected by the doors
traveled (Am.); (GB): travelled ☐ **friendly:** not hostile
warning: danger signal ☐ **move on:** go away ☐ **hunted:** pursued
nowhere to lay his head: no home; to lay, laid, laid
that: what goes on in tourist cabins ☐ **mumbled:** said indistinctly
walked... from: went out ☐ **hastily:** quickly

just inside the door: at the door ☐ **commissary:** cafeteria
looked around: examined the place ☐ **guardian:** guard
stand: counter ☐ **obtaining:** taking
size: dimension
cursory glance: quick look ☐ **while:** but ☐ **sight:** spectacle
check room: *vestiaire* ☐ **unavoidably:** inevitably
taste: preference ☐ **obtruded itself:** interfered ☐ **beguiled:** charmed
fedora: man's hat ☐ **sprightly:** gay ☐ **feather:** *plume* ☐ **readily:** easily
Stetson: large man's hat

the open spaces. Finally he decided on a sturdy grey Homberg which looked as if it would give him good service. With trembling hands he put it on. It fitted. He walked out — in painful, interminable slow motion.

His confidence was partly restored in the next hour by the fact that no one he encountered made references to tourists' cabins. It had been a lean three months for Pat. He had regarded his job as night clerk for the Selecto Tourists Cabins as a mere fill-in, never to be mentioned to his friends. But when the police squad came this morning they held up the raid long enough to assure Pat, or Don Smith as he called himself, that he would be wanted as a witness. The story of his escape lies in the realm of melodrama, how he went out a side door, bought a half pint of what he so desperately needed at the corner drugstore, hitch-hiked his way across the great city, going limp at the sight of traffic cops and only breathing free when he saw the studio's high-flown sign.

After a call on Louie, the studio bookie, whose great patron he once had been, he dropped in on Jack Berners. He had no idea to submit, but he caught Jack in a hurried moment flying off to a producers' conference and was unexpectedly invited to step in and wait for his return.

The office was rich and comfortable. There were no letters worth reading on the desk, but there were a decanter and glasses in a cupboard and presently he lay down on a big soft couch and fell asleep.

He was awakened by Berners' return, in high indignation.

'Of all the damn nonsense! We get a hurry call — heads

for the open spaces: for sporting activities □ **sturdy:** resistant
Homberg: type of man's hat □ **give... good service:** be useful
it fitted: it was his size
walked out: out of the commissary □ **painful:** laborious
in... slow motion: very slowly
confidence: assurance □ **partly restored:** regained in part
encountered: met □ **made references:** talked about
a lean three months: three difficult months financially; lean ≠ fat
regarded: considered □ **clerk:** receptionist
a mere: a simple □ **fill-in:** a short-term job until he found a better one □ **squad:** brigade
held up the raid long enough: stayed, remained long enough

witness: spectator of incident □ **lies in the realm:** belongs to the domain □ **realm:** *royaume* □ **out:** out by □ **half pint:** a quarter of a litre □ **what:** the drink □ **drugstore:** shop
hitch-hiked his way: *fit de l'auto-stop* □ **limp:** paralyzed with fear
sight: cf. to see □ **cops:** policemen □ **breathing free:** feeling free
high-flown: high in the air
bookie: man who takes people's money to bet on horses
patron: client □ **once:** in the past □ **dropped in:** paid a visit
submit: propose □ **caught:** intercepted; to catch, caught, caught
hurried: pressed for time □ **flying off:** on his way
unexpectedly: surprisingly □ **step in:** come in

worth reading: interesting to read □ **decanter:** glass bottle
cupboard: *placard* □ **presently:** soon □ **lay down:** lay on his back □ **couch:** sofa □ **fell:** to fall, fell, fallen
awakened: woken up □ **in high indignation:** very indignant

of all the damn nonsense: what damn nonsense □ **hurry:** urgent

of all departments. One man is late and we wait for him. He comes in and gets a bawling out for wasting thousands of dollars worth of time. Then what do you suppose: Mr. Marcus has lost his favorite hat!'

Pat failed to associate the fact with himself.

'All the department heads stop production!' continued Berners. 'Two thousand people look for a grey Homberg hat!' He sank despairingly into a chair. 'I can't talk to you today, Pat. By four o'clock, I've got to get a title to a picture about a tourist camp. Got an idea?'

'No,' said Pat. 'No.'

'Well, go up to Bee McIlvaine's office and help her figure something out. There's fifty dollars in it.'

In a daze Pat wandered to the door.

'Hey,' said Berners, 'don't forget your hat.'

III

Feeling the effects of his day outside the law, and of a tumbler full of Berners' brandy, Pat sat in Bee McIlvaine's office.

'We've got to get a title,' said Bee gloomily.

She handed Pat the mimeograph offering fifty dollars reward and put a pencil in his hand. Pat stared at the paper unseeingly.

'How about it?' she asked. 'Who's got a title?'

There was a long silence.

'*Test Pilot's* been used, hasn't it?' he said with a vague tone.

'Wake up!This isn't about aviation.'

'Well, I was just thinking it was a good title.'

bawling out: shouting, lamentation □ **wasting:** losing
worth: of value equivalent to
what do you suppose: on top of that
failed to: did not
heads: chiefs, bosses □ **production:** working
Homberg: type of man's hat
sank: collapsed, fell; to sink, sank, sunk □ **despairingly:** with despair in his voice □ **by:** before □ **title:** name
picture: film □ **got an idea:** have you got an idea

go up: go along □ **figure something out:** invent something
in it: as a reward
in a daze: in a state of confusion □ **wandered:** went slowly

outside the law: as a criminal
tumbler: glass □ **sat:** to sit, sat, sat

gloomily: in a depressed tone
handed: gave □ **mimeograph:** copy of the bulletin
reward: recompense □ **stared:** looked fixedly
unseeingly: without seeing it
who's got: who has got

***Test Pilot*:** film by Victor Fleming (1938)

'So's *The Birth of a Nation.*'

'But not for this picture', Pat muttered. '*Birth of a Nation* wouldn't suit this picture.'

'Are you ribbing me?' demanded Bee. 'Or are you losing your mind? This is serious.'

'Sure — I know.' Feebly he scrawled words at the bottom of the page. 'I've had a couple of drinks that's all. My head'll clear up in a minute. I'm trying to think what have been the most successful titles. The trouble is they're all been used, like *It Happened One Night*.'

Bee looked at him uneasily. He was having trouble keeping his eyes open and she did not want him to pass out in her office. After a minute she called Jack Berners.

'Could you possibly come up? I've got some title ideas.'

Jack arrived with a sheaf of suggestions sent in from here and there in the studio, but digging through them yielded no ore.

'How about it, Pat? Got anything?'

Pat braced himself to an effort.

'I like *It Happened One Morning*', he said — then looked desperately at his scrawl on the mimeograph paper, 'or else — *Grand Motel*.'

Berners smiled.

'*Grand Motel*', he repeated. 'By God! I think you've got something. *Grand Motel*.'

'I said *Grand Hotel*', said Pat.

'No, you didn't. You said *Grand Motel* — and for my money it wins the fifty.'

'I've got to go lie down', announced Pat. 'I feel sick.'

'There's an empty office across the way. That's a funny

The Birth of a Nation: film by D.W. Griffith (1915)
muttered: said in an indistinct voice
suit: be adequate
ribbing me: kidding me, making fun of me
losing your mind: losing your head
feebly: without energy □ **scrawled:** wrote badly □ **bottom:** lowest part □ **a couple of:** two
'll: will □ **clear up:** grow clear
the trouble is: the problem is

uneasily: with a disturbed expression □ **trouble:** difficulty

pass out: lose consciousness

a sheaf: a few sheets of paper □ **from here and there:** from various departments □ **digging:** reading □ **yielded:** produced
ore: treasure
got anything: have you got anything
braced himself: prepared himself

scrawl: a few words badly written □ **or else:** *ou alors*
motel: hotel by the roadside

you've got something: you have had a great idea

for my money: as far as I am concerned
fifty: 50 dollars
to go lie down: to go to bed □ **sick:** not well
empty: with nobody in it □ **across the way:** on the other side

idea Pat, *Grand Motel* — or else *Motel Clerk*. How do you like that?'

As the fugitive quickened his step out the door Bee pressed the hat into his hands.

'Good work, old-timer', she said.

Pat seized Mr. Marcus' hat, and stood holding it there like a bowl of soup.

'Feel — better — now', he mumbled after a moment. 'Be back for the money.'

And carrying his burden he shambled toward the lavatory.

quickened his step: walked more quickly □ **out the door:** to get out of the office □ **pressed:** put
old-timer: veteran
seized: took in his hand □ **stood:** to stand, stood, stood

mumbled: said indistinctly
be back: I shall come back
burden: *fardeau* □ **shambled:** walked with difficulty

Grammaire au fil des nouvelles

En traduisant les phrases suivantes au moyen des structures suggérées en italiques entre parenthèses essayez de retrouver le texte anglais dont la page et la ligne sont indiquées par des chiffres : le premier renvoie à la page, le second à la ligne.

On avait retiré les miroirs un an auparavant (*passif ;* **ago**, 156.13).

Pourquoi ne veulent-ils pas remettre des miroirs dans les toilettes ? (**will**, 156.22).

Pensent-ils que les scénaristes passeraient la journée à se regarder ? (*pronom réfléchi,* 156.23).

Bee avait dû voir l'expression de son regard (*modalité,* 156.31).

Soit mon film commence demain soit il est mis au placard (*soit... soit...,* 158.1).

Pat sortit rapidement de la pièce (*préposition,* 158.19).

S'emparer du chapeau d'un étranger comportait une complication (*nominalisation,* 158.26).

Finalement il choisit un chapeau qui semblait pouvoir lui faire de l'usage (*choisir ;* **...looked as if...**, 160.1).

Il le mit avec des mains tremblantes (160.3).

Pat venait de passer trois mois difficiles (160.8).

Il n'y avait pas de lettres intéressantes à lire sur le bureau (**worth** + *gérondif,* 160.26).

Il faut que j'aie un titre avant 4 heures (162.9).

Test Pilot a déjà été utilisé, non ? (**tags**, 162.29).

Il avait du mal à garder les yeux ouverts (164.11).

Elle ne voulait pas qu'il perde conscience dans son bureau (*structure infinitive,* 164.12)

Vocabulaire en contexte

Voici 1300 mots rencontrés dans les nouvelles, suivis du sens qu'ils ont dans celles-ci.

— A —

about to sur le point de
above au-dessus
absently distraitement
abuse insulter
according to d'après, selon
acquaintance connaissance
across à travers
act agir
actually en fait
add ajouter
advice conseil
advise conseiller
afterwards après, plus tard
aggrieved blessé
aghast horrifié
agog excité
ahead en avant, devant
ajar entrebâillé, ouvert
albeit bien que
alike pareil, ressemblant
alimony pension alimentaire
all tout
allot attribuer
alloy alliage
almost presque
alone seul
aloof distant
aloud à haute voix
already déjà
anger colère
angle point de vue, combine
anteroom antichambre
anyhow de toute façon
anywhere n'importe où
apiece chacun, respectivement
apologetically en s'excusant
appeal to faire appel à
apt adéquat, juste
arm bras
arrival arrivée
as for quant à
as if comme si
ascent montée, ascension
ashamed honteux
asleep endormi
assign attribuer
assignment tâche, travail
at large à la cantonade, dans l'ensemble
at length longuement

athwart en face, à l'oblique de
attempt tentative
attorney homme de loi, avocat
avail (with no/to no) en vain
avoid éviter
awaken réveiller
award oneself s'attribuer
aware conscient
away parti

— B —

back dos, dossier
back seat siège arrière
badly vraiment, gravement
bald chauve
ban interdire
ban interdiction
bar interdire
barber shop boutique de coiffeur
bat virée
batch lot, ensemble
bathroom salle de bain
battered usé
bawl out enguirlander
bead goutte
beam sourire gentiment
bean donner un coup
bear, bore, borne appuyer, supporter
beard barbe, barbu
beat, beat, beaten frapper
beckon faire signe
become, became, become devenir
begin, began, begun commencer
beguile charmer, tenter
behave se comporter
behind derrière
bell sonnette, cloche
belong to appartenir à
below dessous, en dessous
bend, bent, bent pencher, se pencher, incliner
bend down se pencher
beside à côté
bet pari
bet parier
betting pari, pari aux courses
between entre
biased partial
big shot gros bonnet
bill billet de banque, facture
bind, bound, bound lier, relier
bitter amer
bitterly amèrement
bland impassible
blandly ironiquement
blank sans expression
blankly sans expression
blink cligner des yeux
blow coup
blow off s'envoler

blow up exploser
body corps
boil bouillir, faire bouillir
bond-salesman vendeur d'obligations
bone os
boo-hoo pleurer, brailler
bookie voir **bookmaker**
bookmaker parieur professionnel
boom shot travelling
born (be) être né
borrow emprunter
both les deux
bother ennuyer, gêner
bother ennui, gêne
bow saluer
box boîte
brace oneself se préparer, rassembler ses forces
brashly avec impudence
break, broke, broken casser
break in pénétrer
break off (s')interrompre
break off s'arrêter
break out éclater
breath haleine, souffle
breathe respirer
briefcase mallette
bright brillant, clair
bring, brought, brought apporter
broach aborder (un sujet)
brood avoir des idées noires
buck dollar
buddy pote
building bâtiment
burden peser
burden fardeau
burn up brûler
business affaires
bust exploser
bustle s'agiter
busy occupé
buttonhole boutonnière
buy, bought, bought acheter
by par, dès

— C —

calendar calendrier
call appel
call appeler
call back rappeler
call in faire appel à
callboy messager, assistant
called for requis, nécessaire
caller visiteur
cannon fodder chair à canon
career carrière
careful prudent
careless négligent
carry porter
cash argent comptant
cast, cast, cast donner un rôle dans un film
cast a look regarder

casually en passant, l'air dégagé
catch, caught, caught attraper
catch on comprendre
catch wind of s'apercevoir
caution prudence
cautiously prudemment
cavalry cavalerie
cell cellule
cell block prison
cement ciment
chairman of the board président du conseil d'administration
chambers bureaux
check vérifier
check marque
check room vestiaire
cheering encourageant
chest poitrine, torse
chiefly surtout
choice choix
choose, chose, chosen choisir
chore corvée
chuckle petit rire
church église
clean propre
clean up nettoyer, arranger
clear up s'éclaircir
clergy clergé
clerk employé
clever intelligent
cloud nuage
clue indice
clutch lever embrayage
coinage néologisme, mot inventé
cold froid
collapse s'effondrer
comb peigne
comb for chercher
come back revenir
come in entrer
commissary cafétéria, restaurant du studio
compete rivaliser
competition concurrence
conceal dissimuler
confidence confiance
confidently avec confiance
contract (under) sous contrat
coo parler d'une voix flûtée
cook up pondre
cool frais
cop policier
copy exemplaire
cosily tranquillement, confortablement
coterie groupe
couch sofa
count compter
couple (a) deux
course golf
cover couverture
crack fissure
crackle craquer, crépiter
crane grue
crayon écrire au crayon

creak grincement
credits générique
creep, crept, crept s'infiltrer, ramper
crisis crise
cross en colère
crowd foule
crowded bondé
crumble s'émietter, se décomposer
cry pleurer
cunning rusé
cup tasse
cure cure
curfew couvre-feu
current actuel
cursory rapide, superficiel
cushion coussin
cut changement de plan
cutaway coat habit

— D —

dab toucher légèrement
dart se précipiter, filer
dash filer comme l'éclair
dashing brillant, élégant
date rendez-vous
daughter fille
dawn aube, lumière
daze (in a) la tête dans les nuages
dazzling éblouissant
dear cher, coûteux
decade décennie
deceased décédé
deed exploit, haut fait
deep profond
deferential poli, plein de déférence
defiantly avec insolence
deliberately en prenant son temps
deliver transmettre
depart partir
department service
desk bureau
despair désespoir
desperate désespéré
desperation désespoir
dig, dug, dug creuser, aller chercher, fouiller
dig up trouver
digest digérer
directions instructions
director metteur en scène
directory annuaire
discard jeter
disclose révéler
disgustedly avec répugnance
dismal sinistre
dispose of se débarrasser de
dissolve fondu, enchaîné
distress détresse, chagrin
disturb gêner, perturber
doggedly avec obstination
dogs pieds
doll poupée

dot parsemer
doubt doute
down to réduit à, jusqu'à
draft gorgée, lampée
drag poids, problème
dramatic spectaculaire
draw, drew, drawn tirer
draw near (s')approcher
draw out faire parler
draw to rest s'arrêter
dream rêve
dreamer rêveur
dreamy rêveur
dressed up déguisé, sur son trente et un
drive, drove, driven conduire
drive away s'éloigner (en voiture)
drop laisser tomber, déposer
drop in rendre visite
drown out noyer
drugstore drugstore, cafétéria
drum up concocter
drunk saoul, ivrogne
duck abandonner

— E —

each other l'un, l'autre/les uns, les autres
eager désireux de, impatient
eagerly avec impatience
eagerness vif désir, impatience
ear oreille
early tôt
earn gagner
earnestly sérieusement
ease facilité
easy-going facile à vivre, indolent
edge bord
edge out pousser en dehors, éclipser
eight-ball boule de billard
either... or soit... soit
elaborate compliqué
elated enthousiaste, euphorique
elbow se frayer un chemin
elbow coude
elderly âgé
else sinon, autre
emergency urgence
emissary émissaire, représentant
empty vide
encounter rencontre
encounter rencontrer
end fin
end finir
ending fin
enlist s'engager
enough assez
ensuing suivant
entrance entrée
era ère, époque

ersatz succédané
escape fuite
even même
even though même si
ever toujours, jamais
exalted distingués
executive dirigeants
exhausted épuisé
expect s'attendre à
extra figurant
eyebrows sourcils

— F —

face visage
facetious facétieux
fade fondu
fade out se fondre
failure raté, échec
faint faible, indistinct
fairly assez, justement
faith foi
fall, fell, fallen tomber
fall asleep s'endormir
fall into step emboîter le pas
fall upon tomber sur, se poser sur
false faux
falter hésiter
far loin, de loin
far between espacé
far-fetched tiré par les cheveux, compliqué
fast rapide
fast rapidement
fate destin
favorite préféré
feather plume
feeble faible
feed, fed, fed nourrir
feel, felt, felt sentir
feeling sentiment
feelingly avec chaleur, avec feu
fellow camarade, collègue
fence palissade, drille
festive joyeux
few peu, rare
fierce féroce
fifth cinquième
fight, fought, fought se battre, combattre
figure out imaginer, inventer
fill remplir
fill-in provisoire
find, found, found trouver
fine bien, beau
fire incendie
first aid premiers secours
first hand (at) de près, en première ligne
fit aller, convenir
fix arranger
fix up arranger
flabbergasted ébahi
flag drapeau
flea puce
flight envol, fuite
fling, flung, flung jeter
flood flot, inondation

floor sol
flow flot, cours
fly, flew, flown voler, se sauver
fly in the ointment problème
fly off se sauver, partir rapidement
fog brouillard
foil faire échouer
folder brochure
follow suivre
following suivant
footstep bruit de pas
for fear of de crainte que/de
forehead front
forestall prendre les devants, prévenir
forget, forgot, forgotten oublier
forgive, forgave, forgiven pardonner
forward en avant
frail fragile
frantic frénétique
frantically frénétiquement
freak excentrique, monstre
free libre, gratuit
freeze out exclure
friendly amical
fright frayeur
frighten effrayer
frisking fouille corporelle
from now on à partir de maintenant
front seat siège de devant
frown froncer les sourcils
fuel combustible, énergie
full plein
fumble tâtonner
further plus loin
further on plus loin

— G —

gag plaisanterie
gallery (art) musée
game jeu
gate grille
gather rassembler, se rassembler
gauge évaluer
gawk regarder bouche-bée
gear oneself se préparer
gently doucement
gesture geste, mouvement
get, got, got (-ten) avoir, obtenir
get along s'entendre
get in entrer
get off descendre
get on continuer
get out sortir
get to arriver
get to one's feet se lever
gift don, cadeau

give a lift déposer en voiture
give up, gave, given abandonner
gizzard cou
glad content
gladness satisfaction
glamorous prestigieux
glance jeter un coup d'œil
glance coup d'œil
glass verre
glazed vitreux
glimpse aperçu, coup d'œil
gloom dépression
gloomily tristement
gloomy sombre, lugubre
glow briller
glow chaleur, lumière
glue colle
go on, went, gone continuer
go places aller loin
grab se saisir de
grand mille dollars
grapple affronter
grateful reconnaissant
gravy ride la bonne soupe
grease paint maquillage
greet saluer
grimly l'air sombre, sinistre
grin léger sourire
grip compréhension, maîtrise
grit one's teeth serrer les dents
groan gémir, se plaindre
grow, grew, grown grandir, croître
gruffly sèchement
grumble marmonner
guess supposition
guess deviner, supposer
guest invité
guild corporation, association
guilt culpabilité
guilty coupable
gulp avaler
guts tripes
guy type
gyp escroc, escroquerie

— H —

hail saluer
hair cheveux
half moitié
hall vestibule
ham acteur (péjoratif)
hand donner
hand (at first) de bonne source
handful poignée
handle donner, tendre
hang, hung, hung accrocher

hang something on someone accuser quelqu'un de quelque chose
hang up raccrocher
happen arriver
hard by tout près
hardship difficulté
hastily avec précipitation
hate haïr
hate haine
hatred haine
have a heart avoir pitié
head tête, chef
headline manchette, gros titre
headlong précipité
health santé
hear of, heard, heard entendre parler de
heart cœur
heartily avec chaleur
heat chaleur
heat wave vague de chaleur
heavy lourd
hedge haie
hell enfer
help aider
hilt garde
hinge gond, pivot
hire employer
hit show spectacle à succès
hitch-hike faire de l'auto-stop
hoarsely d'une voix rauque
hold, held, held tenir, retenir
hold back retenir
hop in sauter dans
hophead drogué
hot chaud
hulk masse, carcasse
hunt chasser
hunted traqué
hurried pressé
hurry presser
hurry (in a) pressé
hurt, hurt, hurt blesser, faire mal
husband mari

— I —

ill mal, malade
impede gêner, bloquer, entraver
imposition imposture
improve améliorer
inconspicuously discrètement
increase augmenter
increasingly de plus en plus
incredulously sans y croire
inquire se renseigner
inside à l'intérieur
instead au lieu de

intersperse entremêler
iron fer

— J —

jack argent (argot)
jacket couverture, veste
jail prison
Jew (a) juif (nom)
Jewish juif (adj.)
johnnies toilettes
joint endroit, établissement
joke plaisanterie
jump sauter

— K —

kick around discuter (un projet)
kid gosse, jeune
kid plaisanter
kind sorte
kitchen cuisine
knock frapper à la porte
knock coup
knock down frapper
knowledge connaissance

— L —

labor(s) travail, labeur
lack manque
lack manquer
land obtenir, “se dégotter”
landlord propriétaire
lapse trou
larceny vol
last durer
last dernier
late en retard
later plus tard
latter dernier
laugh rire
launch lancer, monter
lavatory toilettes
law loi, droit
lawn pelouse
lay, laid, laid étendre, poser
lay down s’allonger
lay out (to) expliquer, disposer
lead, led, led mener
leaf (pl. leaves) feuille
lean se pencher
lean maigre, peu prospère
least (at) du moins
leather cuir
leave, left, left quitter, partir
left over de reste
leisure loisir
leisurely en prenant son temps
level niveau
license permis
lick into shape remanier, corriger

licked tenu en échec, battu
lie mentir
lie, lay, lain être posé, se trouver
lie down s'allonger
lie in résider, appartenir à
lift soulever
light lumière
limp sans forces
lines texte
linger s'attarder
lip lèvre
liquor alcool
loan prêter
loan prêt
locked verrouillé
locution langage
long lost perdu depuis longtemps
look regard
look around visiter
look for chercher
look on, upon donner sur
lose, lost, lost perdre
lose one's grip perdre la main
loss perte
lot studio
lots beaucoup
lousy minable
lower plus bas
luck chance
luncheon déjeuner de midi

— M —

make a pass faire des avances, "draguer"
make someone's acquaintance faire la connaissance de quelqu'un
make use of se servir de
make-up maquillage
male masculin/homme
manage réussir à
manageress patronne
manhood virilité, dignité d'homme
manner attitude
mansion villa de luxe
map carte
market marché
meager maigre
meal repas
mean, meant, meant signifier
meanwhile pendant ce temps
medium shot plan moyen
meet, met, met rencontrer
memory souvenir
mere simple
merge fusionner
messy confus, désordonné
midway à mi-course
mimeographed copié à l'aide d'un stencil
mind esprit, tête

misery malheur, tristesse
misfortune malheur, mésaventure
miss rater
miss a beat s'arrêter de battre
missing absent
mist brume
mixed up impliqué, "embringué"
momentarily momentanément
momentous important
moodily tristement
moody triste, déprimé
motel hôtel sur le bord de la route
motionless immobile
motor voiture
mount monter
mourn gémir, se plaindre
mournful lugubre
move on partir
mud boue
muff barbe
muff barbu
mumble marmonner
mumps oreillons
musing méditations
mutter marmonner

— N —

nag cheval
napkin serviette de table
narrow étroit
nearby proche
need besoin
neighbor voisin
neither... nor ni... ni
nephew neveu
neuritis douleur
never jamais
next prochain
next door voisin
no matter peu importe
no soap pas question
nod hochement de tête
nod hocher la tête
nonentities personnages insignifiants
nor ni
nurse infirmière
nuts fou

— O —

object faire objection
obviously évidemment
occasional occasionnel
odd bizarre
oddly étrangement
off the cuff improvisé
offend offenser
office bureau
often souvent
ominous de mauvais augure
on and off par intermittence
once une fois, autrefois

once upon a time il était une fois
opportunity occasion, chance
or else ou alors
out of hors de
out of sight invisible
out on one's ear jeté dehors
outset début, départ
outside à l'extérieur
over fini
over au-dessus, en plus
over there là-bas
oversell, -sold, sold en faire trop
overstuffed massif
overwhelmed dépassé, ému
own propre, personnel
own posséder
oxfords chaussures

— P —

pace pas, rythme, allure
pack empaqueter
painful douloureux
painting tableau
pan mouvement panoramique de la caméra
pang douleur, sentiment, affres
pant être hors d'haleine
panting hors d'haleine
pants pantalon
part séparer, faire une raie
party groupe, soirée, réception
pass carte d'accès
pass away mourir
pass out perdre conscience, s'évanouir
past passé
paste colle
patron client
payroll (on the) engagé, employé
peanut cacahuète
peep coup d'œil furtif
peep regarder furtivement
peer scruter
pencil écrire au crayon
pencil crayon
people gens
pep up se ressaisir
phoney ringard, minable
phony ringard
pick choisir, prendre
pick out choisir
pick up ramasser
picture se figurer, imaginer
picture film
pinhead idiot
pint demi-litre
piqued vexé
placard affiche
plain simple, laid
play jouer

playwright auteur de théâtre
playwriter auteur dramatique
pleasure plaisir
plot histoire
plump corpulent, bien en chair
plunge plonger, se lancer
point montrer
poised prêt, en position
pole poteau
pool piscine
poop idiot
pour verser, déverser
poverty pauvreté
powder poudre
power pouvoir, puissance
powerful puissant
presently bientôt, maintenant
press release communiqué de presse
pressure pression
pretty joli
pretty bien, plutôt
pretty good pas mal
pride orgueil
prime meilleur, âge d'or
private privé, particulier
privet hedge haie de
proficient bien fait
profusely abondamment
prop boy, prop man accessoiriste
property propriété
prophesy prédire
prospect perspective
proud fier
proxy (by) par procuration
psychoanalyst psychanalyste
pull tirer, boire
pulse pouls
purse pochette, sac de dame
pursue poursuivre
push past repousser
put back remettre
put forward mettre en avant, avancer
put on, put, put mettre
puzzle déconcerter, intriguer

— Q —

quail frémir de peur
Quaker Quaker
quarrel querelle
quarry proie
quaver trembler
question mettre en doute
quicken accélérer
quiet tranquille, calme
quite tout à fait, complètement

— R —

race course
rack étagère
racket combine
radical extrémiste, révolutionnaire
raise augmentation
raise élever, monter
range from... to aller de... à
range (long) longue portée
rather...than plutôt...que
reach atteindre
reach for chercher
read, read, read lire
readily facilement
ready prêt
rear arrière
recognize reconnaître
reconcile réconcilier, concilier
Red Cross Croix-Rouge
redeem racheter
red-rimmed rouge, aux bords rouges
refresh rafraîchir
refurbish réviser, rénover, polir
regard considérer
regard (in that) à cet égard
regular habituel
rehearsal répétition
rehearse répéter
relief soulagement
remain rester
remind rappeler
remnants reste
remove déplacer, enlever, ôter
repair réparation
request demande
resemble ressembler à
rest se reposer
retire prendre sa retraite
reverse inverser
reward récompenser
reward récompense
rib se moquer de
ricketing hésitant, mal assuré
right vrai
right away tout de suite
right down to jusqu'à
rights droits
ring sonnerie
ring, rang, rung sonner
rise, rose, risen se lever, s'élever
roadster décapotable
rock balancer, se balancer
rouse susciter, réveiller
ruffled vexé
run, ran, run courir
run série, passage
runner coureur
rush précipitation, cohue
rush se précipiter
rusty rouillé

— S —

safe en sécurité
safety sécurité, abri
salad days jeunesse, âge d'or
sanguine déterminé
save sauver
scabbard fourreau
scale échelle
scapegoat bouc émissaire
scarcely à peine, rarement
scatter disséminer, éparpiller
scoff se gausser de
scram dégager
scrawl griffonner
screen écran
script scénario
seal sceller
second to none inégalé
second (in a split) en un rien de temps
see, saw, seen voir
seek, sought, sought chercher, rechercher
seem sembler
seize saisir
send for, sent, sent envoyer chercher
sentence phrase
set décor, scène
set down, set, set poser
set fire to mettre feu à
settee sofa
several plusieurs
shack hutte, cabane
shake, shook, shaken trembler, agiter
shake off se débarrasser de
shake-up bouleversement, changement
shamble tituber
shame-faced l'air honteux
sharply durement, sèchement
sheaf liasse
shelf étagère
shelve mettre au placard
shinbone tibia
shine, shone, shone briller
shining reluisant
shiver frisson
shoot, shot, shot filmer, tirer
shoot dice jouer aux dés
shoot out se battre au revolver
shooting script synopsis
short film court ou documentaire
short court
shot coup de feu, plan
shout crier
show, showed, showed/shown montrer
showdown affrontement
shrill perçant
shut, shut, shut fermer
shut up shop fermer boutique

sick malade
sickroom chambre de malade
side côté, bord
side door porte dérobée
sideboard buffet, placard
sidewalk trottoir
sideways de côté, sur le côté
sigh soupirer
sight vue, spectacle
sight of (in) en vue de
sight (by) de vue
sign up embaucher
signal faire signe
silent movies films muets
simmer bouillonner, réduire
sin péché
since depuis, puisque
singe brûler
single unique, célibataire
sink, sank, sunk se laisser tomber, sombrer
sink in pénétrer, être assimilé
size taille
slanting de biais
slap donner une tape
slide se glisser
slightly légèrement
slip bout
slip se glisser
slit couper
slow down ralentir
smacker dollar
smart intelligent, élégant
smile sourire
snag piège, "hic"
snap se briser
sniff renifler
so far jusqu'ici
soak tremper
soar monter
socko verve, sentiment
soften adoucir
softly doucement
soiled souillé, sale
solid important
somewhat quelque peu
soul âme
sound sonner, résonner
sound bruit, son
sound le parlant
speak, spoke, spoken parler
speech discours
speechless muet
spirit esprit
split up répartir, diviser
spot déceler
sprawl s'étendre, être affalé
spread étendre, s'étendre
sprightly gai, pimpant, fringant
spring bond
spring, sprang, sprung sauter, jaillir
squad brigade
squirt malotru, blanc-bec
stage scène
staircase cage d'escalier
stairs escalier

stamp timbre
stand comptoir
stand up, stood, stood se lever
stand, stood, stood être debout
star étoile
stare regarder fixement
starry-eyed l'air émerveillé
start sursaut
start sursauter
start off démarrer
startling étonnant
state of things état de choses
statement déclaration
stay demeurer, rester
steal, stole, stolen voler
steaming fumant
step pas, démarche
step in entrer
stick around rester dans les parages
stick, stuck, stuck coller
still encore, pourtant
stinking puant
stir remuer
stirred up excité
stock troupe, réserve, "écurie"
stock ticker cours de la Bourse par télex
stockholders actionnaires
stomach estomac
straight droit, directement
straight to droit à, droit vers
streak filet
streamlined aérodynamique
street car tramway
strength force
stress tension
stretch s'étendre
strike grève
strike (on) en grève
strike, struck, struck/stricken frapper
strip bout, feuille
stripe rayure
striped rayé
strong fort
struggle lutte
stuff trucs, choses, histoires
stuffed shirt rabat-joie, collet monté
stun abasourdir
sturdy solide, résistant
submit soumettre
sucker idiot, naïf
sucker-trap piège à gogo
suddenly soudain
suit convenir, convenir à
suitable correct, convenable, adéquat
summary résumé
superciliously avec mépris
supply fournir
surrounded entouré
survey étudier, observer

suspicious suspect, soupçonneux
swagger vantardise, fatuité
swallow avaler
swallow gorgée
swarm grouiller
swell formidable
swift rapide
swiftly rapidement
swimming-pool piscine
swing, swung, swung se balancer
switch off éteindre
switch on allumer
sympathetic compatissant

— T —

tablet comprimé
take, took, taken prendre
take a step faire un pas, prendre une décision
take away emporter, ôter
take care of s'occuper de
take off ôter
take place avoir lieu
take the rap être tenu pour responsable
talkies films parlants
talking pictures films parlants
tall haut, grand
task tâche
team équipe
team up collaborer
tear larme
tearful avec des sanglots dans la voix
tell, told, told dire, raconter
test bout d'essai, essai
then alors, puis, donc
thick épais
thin mince, peu abondant
think, thought, thought penser
think up imaginer
thirsty assoiffé
thirty trente
thought pensée
thoughtfully pensivement
threaten menacer
through à travers
throw, threw, thrown jeter, lancer
throw up vomir
throw up produire
thrust, thrust, thrust lancer, se lancer
tide over dépanner
tied up lié
till jusqu'à
timely opportun
tip tuyau, pourboire
tire (tyre) pneu
tired fatigué
title titre
toil labeur
Tommy gun petite mitraillette

tooth (pl. teeth) dent(s)
top haut
tough dur
tough customers "durs"
tour visite
tourist cabin bungalow de vacances
toward vers
towel serviette
track piste de champ de courses
traffic circulation
trail piste
training formation
tramp vagabond
trash qui ne vaut rien
travel voyager
tray plateau
treatment synopsis
trim couper, tailler
tripe sornettes, stupidités
trucking shot travelling vertical
true vrai, fidèle
trust faire confiance
trusted de confiance
truth vérité
try essayer
tumbler grand verre
tuna fish thon
turn tourner
turn around se tourner
turn out s'avérer
turn up se présenter
twirp idiot
type (in) imprimé
typescript scénario tapé à la machine
typewriter machine à écrire

— U —

ubiquitous omniprésent
ukase ordre
umbrella parapluie
under sous
understand, -stood, -stood comprendre
uneasily mal à l'aise
uneasy inquiet
unfailingly sans coup férir
union syndicat
unless à moins que
unprosperous pauvre, dans la gêne
until jusqu'à
unwillingly contre son gré
unwisely imprudemment
unworried serein
up to jusqu'à
up to it à la hauteur, capable
up (something is) quelque chose se passe
useless inutile
utter émettre, prononcer

— V —

valuable précieux
venture hasarder
very même
very très
vineyard vigne
vivid animé, brillant

— W —

wager pari
wagon petite voiture
wait attendre
waiting room salle d'attente, antichambre
waitress serveuse
wake, woke, woken (s')éveiller
walk trottoir, allée
walk marcher
wall mur
wander errer, marcher lentement
wangle obtenir, décrocher
wants besoins
war guerre
warm chaud
warm to s'enthousiasmer pour
warning avertissement
waste gaspiller
watch over surveiller
watch (on) de garde
wawe vague
way up bien au-dessus
way (in the) qui encombre, de trop
way (that) comme cela
way (on the) en projet
weak faible
weakly faiblement
wear, wore, worn porter
wearily l'air fatigué, las
wee minuscule
week semaine
weeper pleureur
well-known célèbre
wet humide
whenever à chaque fois que
whereupon sur quoi
wherever où que ce soit
whether si
while tandis que
while moment
whipped battu
whiskers favoris, moustaches
whistling sifflant
whole entier
wife (pl. wives) épouse
wig perruque
wild effrayé
wild sauvage
wildly avec l'énergie du désespoir
willowy mince
win, won, won gagner
wince faire la grimace
wind vent
windshield pare-brise

wink clin d'œil
wink faire un clin d'œil
winter hiver
wire télégramme
wistfully avec nostalgie
within à l'intérieur
within range à portée de
witness témoin
wonder se demander
wonderful merveilleux
wont habitude
word mot, nouvelle
work out percer à jour
worry inquiétude
worry se faire du souci
worth valeur
worthy valable
wrestling lutte
wrist poignet
write, wrote, written écrire
wrong faux, injuste, mal

— Y —

yell hurler
yellow jaune
yet cependant, encore
yield donner, céder
yield rendement
youth jeunesse, jeune

Composition réalisée par COMPOFAC - PARIS

IMPRIMÉ EN FRANCE PAR BRODARD ET TAUPIN
Usine de La Flèche (Sarthe).
LIBRAIRIE GÉNÉRALE FRANÇAISE - 6, rue Pierre-Sarrazin - 75006 Paris.

ISBN : 2 - 253 - 04691 - 8 30/8604/8